"ADVENTURE, SUSPENSE AND JUST GOOD FUN"

—**Dallas News**

"Excitement, plot . . . once started the ball of adventure becomes a rolling stone . . . the young professor does enough first-hand research in the underworld to satisfy anybody . . ."

—**Chicago Tribune**

"Well plotted, exceptionally well written, provocative."

—**Los Angeles News**

"MR. WYLIE MEANT TO ENTERTAIN. AND HE SUCCEEDS BEAUTIFULLY."

—**Houston Post**

PUT PLEASURE IN YOUR READING

LARGER TYPE MAKES THE DIFFERENCE

This Easy Eye Edition is set in large clear type— at least 30 percent larger than the usual paperback book. It is printed on scientifically tinted non-glare paper for better contrast and less eyestrain.

PHILIP WYLIE
EXPERIMENT IN CRIME

LANCER
LANCER BOOKS  EDITIONS
NEW YORK

EXPERIMENT IN CRIME

One:

A RINGING denunciation of crime was responsible for the entrance of Professor Martin Luther Burke into the demimonde. More accurately, the challenge of a lovely young lady precipitated the event. And the weather had something to do with it.

Men's lives are often—and fittingly—compared with the courses of rivers: one life is a noisy torrent, another is a lazy meander, and a third is a mere tributary. Some rivers flow inconspicuously for great distances only to encounter a geological fault that turns them abruptly into crashing falls and bellowing cataracts. So it was with Professor Burke.

For his first six years he had merely grown, an undersized and unnoteworthy lad in a New England village—a mere rill. For seventeen years, he had thereafter studied—a small stream growing with the volume of knowledge. He had been an instructor after that, teaching sociology and psychology. Full professorship was accorded him in his thirtieth year, after a wartime interlude in which his forte had been disregarded by the Army and his knowledge of languages had been exploited.

He had censored endless thousands of letters written by homesick G.I.s in other tongues than English. His collected lectures had been published. Now, as a professor of socio-psychology at the University of Miami, his course in life, like the courses he taught, seemed certain to flow serenely—a river without dash, a river that neither floods nor dries up, that scarcely changes even when it freezes.

The trouble was the weather, to start with.

It was an unsuitable day for scholarship. A warm haze hung over the land and sunlight filtered through it, lying on the lush vegetation like melted butter. Birds sang alluringly. A clump of bushes, planted directly under the windows by a thoughtless landscape architect, sent into the lecture room an unsettling perfume. It was bad enough for the young lady students to wear commercial fragrances with names like Tumult and Triple-Dare; that nature should conspire in the fashion was all but intolerable.

Professor Burke paused in his lecture on Crime and Civic Corruption. "Greater Miami," he said, "unfortunately furnishes a cross section of the socio-psychological ailments under discussion." As usual, the mention of their own region instilled new interest among the students. "In this resort area the demand for what is called diversion reaches a nadir. The gambler, the bookmaker, the racketeer and the vice overlord line the pockets of the politician for illegal protection. I refer you here to *Studies in Antisocial Organisms* by Waite and Treachness, which contains a masterly chapter on South Florida . . ."

As he dissertated upon Waite and Treachness, his own eye wandered to the window and the green world beyond. MacFalkland was just passing—on a bicycle—golf bag jingling on his back and his hirsute chest showing through the open triangle of a rather loud sports shirt. MacFalkland had no four o'clock class. It was one bit of evidence—a chip in a large mosaic—which made Professor Burke sure that not he, but MacFalkland, was destined to be made Head of the Socio-Psychology Department, when there were funds enough for its establishment. Professor Burke found in a corner of his brain the unwelcome reflection that MacFalkland looked as if he still had several decades of teaching in him. He shook off the mordant idea.

"The criminal," he heard his voice assert, "is an intellectual defective. His crimes are evidence of the fact of his psychological inferiority. You might note down the phrase." They noted it down while he glanced at his own typed manuscript. Vacation would be along soon, and he, too, could wing golf balls into the sunshine for three weeks. He wished he had MacFalkland's shoulders. "The man guilty of corrupting the body politic is, essentially, lacking in imagination and logic. He saws off the limb which sustains him. Crime is identical with the lack of intelligence."

He glanced at his watch. He had one minute of

lecture left—and twelve minutes of class time. He wound up his ringing denunciation—and banished hope, among those who imagined they might be dismissed early, by an old ruse:

"Any questions, ladies and gentlemen?"

A hand went up. The hand of Miss Marigold Macey. In spite of her campus-belle appearance, in spite of the frame of curls which seemed to escape her upswept brown locks by accident, and in spite of the further fact of her good marks, Miss Macey had a way of asking rather sharp questions.

"Yes, Miss Macey?"

She stood up politely. Standing, even in blouse, skirt, and low-heeled shoes, she was still unstudentlike. A little older than the other girls, for one thing. Her education had been interrupted by work having to do with the Red Cross. Several of his male students were as old as she, and even older—for a similar reason: the War.

"I was wondering, Professor Burke, if you were acquainted with any gamblers, racketeers, vice overlords, and so on?" Her voice had a New England accent—although he understood her parents had lived in Florida for more than a decade.

"I fail to see the relevance of the question," he said firmly.

She picked up her notebook and flipped pages. She sounded apologetic. "Last October—in your lecture on the Techniques of the Socio-Psychologist, you said this: 'The true student accepts no theory *per se* and takes no hearsay evidence; he tests every assertion against his own experience in society; he investigates for himself.' " She closed the notebook. "That's what you said. I took it down in shorthand. Naturally, I wondered how much testing and investigating you had done—to lecture about crime."

Professor Burke flushed slightly. His class was amused. "At the time," he said, "I was discussing public health, sanitation, slums, and so on. I hardly feel that such advice may be construed as urging association with criminals."

"I see," the girl said. She did not sit down.

"Was there another question?"

She nodded. "In November," she said, and he bridled a little at her accuracies, "you advised us to read a book called *Social Non-Norms*, by Ledbetter, Shrieben and Morissey. I read it—all eight hundred pages. And *they* say a criminal is sometimes a person of superior intellectual ability who cannot stand the restrictions imposed upon everybody for the sake of mediocrities. They say that *brains* may thus lead to crime—rather than stupidity . . ."

Professor Burke made a mental note never again to recommend any book which he, himself had found too dull, ponderous and turgid for thorough perusal. He had skipped that part, evidently. But he did not like mutiny in his classes. He cleared his throat. "In my opinion, Ledbetter, Shrieben

9

and Morissey erred in their appraisal of that particular subject. They worked carelessly, from inadequate material and false premises—"

"Shrieben," Miss Macey interrupted, "spent two years in the Capone organization in Chicago . . ."

He had forgotten that, too. "A romantic," he said, "rather than a scientist. Shrieben mistook cunning for true intelligence. Every holder of an ordinary degree of Bachelor of Arts is the mental superior of any criminal."

Another hand went up—the hand of Wally Stratton, formerly of the Eighth Air Force and currently of the Football Squad. Obviously, he intended to go to the defense of the physically nubile but mentally thorny Miss Macey.

"Mr. Stratton?"

"Wouldn't it be an interesting idea to get some gangster in here, to debate the matter?"

Professor Burke saw his opening. "Any gambler, or gangster, or other such person among your associates would be welcome here, Mr. Stratton." The class laughed.

Mr. Stratton sat down rather sheepishly. Professor Burke made his usual pre-vacation speech—wishing all of them a pleasant trip home, a safe return, and an interlude of Merry Christmas combined with Happy New Year. He repeated that he hoped none of them would use his course as an excuse for turning to crime: the faculty would disapprove, he ventured.

Several of them came forward to return his greetings and wishes. Among them was Miss Macey, who had to wait while Miss Orme extracted from the professor the titles of books to read over the vacation period. He glared at her ensnooded hair—which always reminded him of a beaver's tail—and gave her the toughest list he could think of. She would eat it up, he thought morosely.

Miss Macey shook his hand and said, "Merry Christmas! Stay out of pool halls and don't pitch pennies!"

He picked up his lecture, remembered he had forgotten his hat, and walked slowly from the long chamber.

Two:

SOME MOMENTS later Mr. Stratton overtook Miss Macey on the palm-lined thoroughfares of Coral Gables.

"Sip, drip?" he asked.

"Sure, boor."

They turned in the direction of a drugstore. "That Burke," he said, "shoe-horned himself out of a hole with a crack at me. Cheap trick. You had him surrounded."

Her brown eyes performed a small minuet. "I was investigating. All fall, I've wondered how much of Martin Burke was theory—and how much was experience."

"Why didn't you ask me? I know the type. Pure brass before a class—and outside, pure mouse. When their mothers look in their mouths to see if, maybe, there's a silver spoon, they find a bookmark. I bet he never got five paces away from an encyclopedia in his life!"

"He's cute," she said demurely.

"Cute!" Mr. Stratton bridled. "That dodo cute?"

"If he's a dodo," she said, stopping to pick a blossom from a city-owned hibiscus, "the best years of your life are shot, too, Wally. He can't be more than thirty-four."

"He was born at least twenty-eight, which is my age. How a dame can see anything in such a oiseau . . . !"

She fixed the flower in her hair. It was reddish brown and salmon. It matched her skirt and did no harm to her skin and her eyes. "He's such a pleasant contrast to the average American male—like you—always leering down rudely from among the chandeliers. A small girl such as me resents the effect of modern nutrition. She feels as if she is dating stepladders all the time."

"Flooey," said Mr. Stratton, who was six-four. "When the moon comes pouring up from the Gulf Stream, do you think about some tame rabbit like Burke? Some one-watt theory-maker? Does he set the petite pulse bouncing?"

"That's what I've wondered all autumn."

"You'd be throwing yourself at a human hamster."

He pushed open the drugstore door. A blast of undergraduate clatter rushed out with the conditioned air. They entered the soda fountain of youth and he pointed to a vacant booth. "Park, lark."

"Delighted, benighted."

"And no more sighing over the professor. As soon as I tap a waitress, I am going to work on you, myself—"

"He gives me maternal feelings," she said, as he began waving his arm, "which mother wouldn't recognize as such. Sometimes I wish I were the local type—Southern, coy, extroverted. I would lead him astray—slightly . . ."

The object of this mild controversy made his way along Pondosa Boulevard and turned into Philomel Court. He turned again into West Cortez Circle. Some boys, playing baseball in a vacant lot, cracked out a hard hit which caromed off a lemon tree, whistled through a plumbego hedge, and rolled toward the sidewalk. Professor Burke ran forward automatically, fielded the ball adeptly, held it until the runner had made a well-earned circuit of the coconut bases, and threw it to the shouting pitcher. He walked on, grinning.

A man slightly under medium size, with a tendency to stoop. A man with eyes now blue and now grey—now steely or ironical and again soft, or vague. A man whose dark hair was worn in a wavy pompadour—an expedient arrangement that exposed all of a rather high forehead. A conventional dresser—in polished brogues, heather socks, gabardine slacks, a light-weight tweed coat, a dimly striped shirt and a conservative blue tie, fixed with a plain gold clip. The stem of a pipe showed in one pocket; from the other, his folded lecture protruded.

Nine strangers out of ten would have confidently guessed that he was a college professor. If they had seen him field the home run they would have added that he was a good egg—and at peace with the world.

Professor Burke was a good egg, insofar as scholastic tradition permitted him good-eggishness. He had New England virtues and a New England conscience. His character and life direction were well established, before he entered the First Grade, by the firm-minded Congregationalists who had been his parents. At thirty-three, he was exactly the way he expected to be at fifty, save that he hoped by then to be a Department Head. He had self-assurance, calm, and a near-fanatical courage of an occasional conviction. He was shy.

At the moment, however, he was not at peace.

He turned into the rather jungly lawn of the house where he had dwelt since his arrival in Miami, after the war. He stumbled on its front steps —which was unusual. He put the wrong key in the lock of the door to his upstairs apartment.

"Martin!" his landlady called. "What's wrong? I'm on the side porch having tea. Scones, too. Come aboard!"

Bedelia Ogilvy was the widow of a retired Naval officer who had quietly passed away in his bed before Pearl Harbor—an event which would certainly have brought him to a more violent demise. Occasionally, Bedelia used such terms as, "Come aboard." She was said to be the homeliest woman in Coral Gables; she was certainly the best cook in that flower-spangled suburb. She had taken Professor Burke very dubiously, and on probation, as a roomer-boarder. After three weeks, she had begun using his first name. After three months, he had commenced unconsciously to regard her

15

as a sort of relative whose pleasure at feeding him superbly was as normal as her constant cross-questioning, anent his mail, his friends, his students, other professors, their wives, and such further lore as might interest her.

He walked around to the side porch, opened the screen, and ducked under the spiny arms of the bougainvillaea. Bedelia sat like a resting camel, behind a rattan coffee table. Her august and bony frame filled the settee. Her large, pale eyes, enlarged further by spectacles, seemed worried. "What's the matter? You're skittish. I can tell."

He knew she could. He did not even try to guess the criteria by which she had detected his nervousness at the distance of thirty-odd feet. "Hypocrisy," he said glumly.

"Hypocrisy? My dear man! The world's full of it! Take it in your stride!"

"My own."

An alert look came into her eyes. "Yours, Martin?"

He told her. He told her his basic advice to his students and of Miss Macey's probing. His eyes even glimmered with appreciation of his predicament. "There I stood—parroting a dozen authorities on criminology—and preaching direct experience—yet I never so much as met a pickpocket face to face in my life! It's absurd!"

"You are hardly expected to be everything you discuss."

"A point I tried to suggest. I fell rather flat. We

were not prepared, in Israel Putnam Teacher's College, for the present postwar generation." He sighed and popped a scone into his mouth.

"Break the next one in two," Bedelia said absently. "I've heard you mention Miss Macey before. Attractive, isn't she? I noticed her picture in the paper when she was elected a sorority president."

"Very attractive." He skipped hurriedly over the fact and railed at the modern student: "Married and with children! In business! Working at places like race tracks! One of our students is a hatcheck girl in a night club—not in my classes, I'm relieved to say. No, Bedelia. We were not prepared for leadership on campuses where the world—the nonacademic world—pushes in at every door. I felt extremely inadequate today. I questioned myself. What right have I—after all —to invite my students to sup at the wellsprings of experience—and to reject them for myself? It's snobbishness, in a way. I felt tempted . . ." he broke off.

"Tempted, Martin? How?" She seemed to relish the idea that he was tempted by anything.

"Well—I can hardly say how. Here we live —in the very midst of a world we never encounter. We read of it in the papers. We learn of it in sociological texts. But the University Campus is as far from the gay life of, say, Miami Beach, as if an ocean lay between—instead of a bay crossed by three causeways. I lecture on gambling. But I

17

have never observed the fact. I was tempted to take precedent in my hands—and go and see."

"Why not?" she asked quickly.

His iced tea halted in mid-air, as if by an invisible brake. "I scarcely expected such a reaction from you!"

Bedelia balanced jam on the remnants of a scone. "Martin, did it ever occur to you that a man can become stuffy—by not resisting stuffiness?"

"Stuffy? A harsh term, Bedelia."

"Why don't you put on your dinner clothes, Martin, and drive over to the Beach and watch some genuine, illegal gambling. You might even see a gangster."

"Because," he answered, obviously wishing the subject had never reached that point, "I haven't the price of a costly meal in my pocket. I would hardly indulge in gambling. And I would hardly patronize such a place with no such intentions. Finally"—he smiled with satisfaction—"I wouldn't have the faintest idea of where to go!"

"The Club Egret," she said, "which is off Collins, at the north end of the Beach. Mrs. Witherspoon told me Wednesday that she lost a hundred and twenty dollars there, the night before. It was probably ten dollars. I have some cash—and you can give me a check. I've kept cash in the house ever since I first moved here. Went to the bank to get the money for a rail ticket and found it was Lee's Birthday! I drew out a hundred dollars the

18

following morning—and I keep it on tap. No telling what obscure Southern heroes might close the banks, I thought—and how was I to remember the date of Lee's Birthday?"

"Really, Bedelia," he said uneasily, "it's most kind. But I wouldn't think of it."

Her face took on an expression of sympathetic contradiction.

Three:

HE DID not know whether he was elated or depressed. The long drive from Coral Gables across the luminous causeway to Miami Beach was exhilarating but not reassuring. He had previously been swimming at Miami Beach. He had played golf there on occasion. He had never visited it at night—and at night the homes seemed richer and more mysterious—the streets strange and a little confusing. The hotels were altogether startling: bathed in colored light—fretted and fringed from top to bottom in cascades of electric glitter. It was opulent and it was ominous.

He located the Club Egret—and drove past it. The Club Egret was boldly set amidst showy residences. It had no windows. Under its portico, attendants were serving the owners of vehicles which markedly outshone his prewar, hand-repainted coupé. Conscience urged him both ways. To enter was folly; not to enter after being committed, was weak. He drove around the block and under the portico.

An obviously disenchanted attendant handed a parking check to him. He gave the man a quarter and received audible thanks. He walked up a flight of stairs.

He found himself in a foyer. There was a checkroom at his left—and a curtained hall—guarded, apparently, by two men in tuxedoes. Straight ahead was a bar—long and shimmering—low lighted—with tables and people at the tables. Men in sports coats—in plain suits—and a few, he saw with relief, in dinner jackets. Overhead was a rosy, vaulted dome. To his right were steps going down—into a tremendous dining room where people in twos and sixes and twenties were busily consuming dinner. The dining room had grey walls with chromium trimmings, a thick, grey carpet, and glass stars in its ceiling; behind each star was a colored light. A large orchestra played rhythmically on a podium. People were dancing. The polychromatic stars twinkled in what seemed to be orchestral tempo. It was dim in the room. The expanse of white tablecloths, the gleaming dance floor, the lofty ceiling and stellar lights, made the professor think of the snowcape under a Christmas tree, expended magically, so that human beings could walk into it.

The headwaiter came forward. "One?"

Professor Burke was escorted into the shimmering, theatrical wonderland. He was seated along the wall.

"Something to drink?"

"A martini. Very dry."

Professor Burke was familiar with the best dining places of Boston. One of these had a bar that turned like a merry-go-round. He was familiar with night clubs through rare visits to the motion pictures. A single cocktail was his limit. However, he knew a good martini from a fair one. He was served a martini he regarded as excellent.

He ordered dinner. He began to look, covertly but searchingly, at the people around him. He thought of them in terms of the textbooks and newspaper articles. They were largely—he felt—gamblers, gangsters, corrupt politicians, labor czars squandering the dues of union members, ladies of the evening, and the like. It would have surprised him a good deal—and disappointed him even more—had he realized that nearly all the men and women were respectable citizens of, or visitors to Miami Beach enjoying an evening of dining and dancing—and not even planning to gamble.

When he cut an excellent filet mignon—for which he would pay a shocking seven dollars—he beckoned the headwaiter. "Where is the gaming room?"

The phrase was not the ordinary one. And it was not customary of newcomers to ask that information of the headwaiter. "You—oh—have not been here before, sir?"

"No, I haven't."

The headwaiter said, "Quite so," and walked away, leaving the professor deeply embarrassed.

The office of Mr. William Sanders was paneled in cypress. In these walls were slots from which the two principal chambers of the Club Egret could be discreetly surveyed. The room also contained a powerful wall safe, expensive, modernistic furniture, and Mr. Sanders himself—a very tall man, lanky, and pleasant. His smile was ready, almost constant; his voice quiet and amiable. One needed, as a rule, a second glance to note that his eyes had a quality like the blade of an adze—seen edge-on.

There was a knock on his door.

Mr. Sanders glanced up from his desk. He said nothing. The door opened and a man entered— a thick-shouldered man with black hair parted in the middle and black eyes of the sort called liquid. The term connotes fluidity and warmth. There was nothing warm about The Tip. If there ever had been, it had turned to ice years before, during The Tip's childhood on the streets of South Chicago.

Mr. Sanders still said nothing.

"There is a laddie-boy outside whose looks I dislike." The Tip touched the ruby-red bow above his soft evening shirt. "Table eighty-six. Are you sure, Double-O, that you have all the dope on tonight's operations?"

Perhaps six people in the world called Mr. Sanders "Bill." Possibly twenty people called him "Double-O" to his face. Thousands, however, used that name when he was not present—though they called him "Mr. Sanders" when they accosted him. Newspapers, also, referred to him on frequent occasions as "Double-O" or "Double-O Sanders."

He regarded The Tip with a smile. The Tip's words showed not the slightest trace of Chicago's streets or even its universal nasal register. The Tip spoke in pure American Park Avenue—an eastern accent which, itself an imitation, is readily copied by anyone who is willing to practice affectation. Smooth phoniness amused Double-O. He answered the question.

"Who's ever positive he has all the dope, in this town? Tonight's operations are set—sure. What's wrong with the guy?"

"Just—keeps looking the place over. The customers. Could be a new Fed income-tax snooping. He asked Rudolph where the 'gaming room' was. Sounds too sappy to be solid. If he is a Fed, he's outsmarting himself."

Double-O crossed to one of the discreet slots, his long legs moving like jointed crowbars. He peered. "I see what you mean," he said, after a while. "I'm willing to bet he's a husband with a wife at a hen convention—afraid somebody he knows will see him here. But tell Connie, anyhow."

Professor Burke ordered coffee and a cigar. He was pleased by the pulchritude of the cigarette girl—and startled by her costume. Hardly enough clothing, he thought, for a large doll. He tipped her a quarter and lighted the cigar. Like every-

24

thing else in the establishment, it was of superlative quality. He blew smoke.

He was filled with a sentiment of self-satisfaction. The fact was that he liked the Club Egret. The fact also was that, even while he enjoyed the music and the lights and the spectacle of the people, he was contriving a few sentences to slip into his next year's lecture—sentences which would make it plain that he had personally investigated the dens of iniquity and found them a tinselly sham.

The house lights went down. A master of ceremony took possession of a microphone—in a cone of smoke-washed light. The professor recognized the first joke as almost identical with one which had been used by Plautus, a little more than two thousand years before.

A girl said, "Hello!"

He turned with surprise—and some discomfiture. The young lady, not identifiable in the dark, was standing at his side.

"May I sit down?" she asked in a warm, husky voice.

"Why, certainly. Of course!"

The professor hurried to assist her. She had long, blonde hair, done up beautifully. Her arms and shoulders were bare, as if she had swum part of her way out of her evening dress. The dress itself winked, and glistened. Her nose turned up slightly. That was all he could discern—excepting

25

that she wore a perfume which had a stunning effect—as a spray has a stunning effect on an insect.

The professor felt slightly guilty, and the resultant course of his thoughts was to be expected. There are some men whom no women, however predatory, however young and inexperienced or old and desperate, will try to pick up. Instinct warns them that the attempt would be futile from every viewpoint. Professor Burke was the archetype of that species of man. And, since no such effort had been made in his case, he suspected none now. He assumed, instead, that the young lady was a former student of his, or a former undergraduate—and that, having recognized him, she had ingratiated herself out of the common, feminine love for scandal. It was, of course, scandalous for him to be dining at the Club Egret.

"My name," said the lady, "is Connie Maxson."

He failed to place it—which in no way surprised him. It usually took him a semester to learn the names of his students—and he seldom remembered them long.

"Would you like coffee? Or a drink?" he asked resignedly.

"Love one."

He beckoned. The lady ordered Scotch and water. After reflection, he said, "The same."

"Enjoying yourself?" she asked.

He raised his eyebrows and blew smoke in an

ironical manner—hoping she would be able to read the gesture. "You would hardly expect a professor of socio-psychology to enjoy himself here. Say rather, I am enjoying the spectacle of a rich, moronic element indulging in pleasures which deprive the body politic of integrity."

The girl said, "Well!" After a moment she asked, "On a vacation?"

"I drove over from the Gables, naturally. Vacation doesn't start for several more days. This is in essence a research project. I'd even intended to watch the gambling for a while. Possibly to squander a few dollars as a sort of payment-in-kind for the experience. The headwaiter, however, was rather huffy about my inquiry."

The house lights went on suddenly.

The girl was extremely beautiful—and the professor was sure he had never seen her before in his life. He would have remembered the face, even if not the name. She was staring at him. She ignored the tango artistes who now appeared on the dance floor.

"Is that straight?" she asked.

"I'm afraid," he said, coloring a little, "that we don't know each other, after all. I assumed you'd been one of my students at the University of Miami."

The drinks came. She made a feint at a toast, sipped, and said, "No, professor. I'm a—sort of hostess—around here. I went to college in the north for one dismal year. Couldn't stand it. Came back here—and couldn't stand the family, either. Gin rummy on the even nights and backgammon on the odd. I—took a job."

"My name is Burke—Martin Burke."

"And you were just looking around?"

He explained in some detail. She was amused, surprised—and, somehow, pleased.

"You're certainly right!" she said. "You shouldn't lecture without background. Now, I tell you. When you're ready, I'll see that you get into the gambling room. If you want, perhaps I can fix it up for you to meet Double-O."

"You mean the notorious Double-O Sanders?"

"He's a lamb, really! Strictly a gambler. No rackets and no other angles. Some of the most important people in the United States come in, regularly." Miss Maxson finished her highball. "I've got to leave now. Thanks for the drink. Ask for Al in the foyer—and he'll show you to the"—she smiled—"'gaming room.'"

Four:

HE THOUGHT—along Tennysonian lines—that she was a delightful creature. He found himself also repeating—along undergraduate lines—that she was a warm swarm. He watched her move among the tables until she was out of view.

Then he called for his check, paid it, tipped ten per cent, added fifty cents, and beckoned to the girl in doll-clothing for another cigar. A corridor led to the gambling room. Al held back the velvet curtain and the professor sauntered through.

He found himself entering a most luxurious room—a room with a lower ceiling and restrained decoration. There were three roulette tables, a cashier's window, two tables surrounded by men, troughlike affairs in which dice were bounding, and other games with which he was unfamiliar. Large floor vases of beige roses were set about. The air was cool and clear, in spite of the continual smoking of its hundred or so occupants. It was like an elegant drawing room—with this exception, he thought: the guests were hypnotized.

They stood around the tables, light reflected up into their faces from the green baize, the polished mahogany. Some were obviously nervous—

their hands toyed with chips or twisted handker-chiefs. Some were strenuously nonchalant. Some were stoical and without expression. The women, he thought, seemed more eager and anxious than the men—a natural result of their more emotional natures. There were women of sixty—even seventy —in fur wraps, wearing jewels. There were young women, with and without jewels. The most con-tinuous sound was the soft talk of the croupiers. The loudest sound was the clatter of fortune set up by the dance of the ivory pellets around the rims of surging wheels.

For a long time, he watched. No one spoke to him—no one seemed to mind his surveillance. He presently realized that there were other on-lookers. He studied the game. Roulette, he soon saw, was childishly simple. Hardly more complex than parcheesi.

He was not in the least tremulous when he went to the cashier's window and purchased twenty, two-dollar, or white, chips. His face was impas-sive when he returned to the table he had selected. He put two chips on Red. The wheel spun and the number was called. The croupier put two chips on his two. He left them where they were. After the next spin, he had eight.

He thought of a number. The number he thought of was nine. He put four chips on nine and four on black. Nine lost. He tried again. Nine came up. He was dumbfounded by the number of chips which were pushed into his possession.

It may be that the best system for winning at gambling is to play with the sincere purpose of losing—of losing a politely decent sum so that (for example) in future years one may warn one's classes, with a little personal anecdote as an illustration, against the folly of betting on the turning of a wheel. In any event, Professor Burke won. He soon noticed that some of his intent associates were waiting until he placed his bets—and following suit. He began to be embarrassed by the size of his pile of chips. He exchanged some for what he called "counters" of a higher denomination. He thought up numbers—and then deliberately bet on others, with the firm intention of defeating himself.

He did not know how long he stood there. An hour, perhaps. It might have been two. He felt a hand on his shoulder and turned shamefacedly. It was Miss Maxson again.

"You're doing peachy, Professor!"

"I'm mortified."

"Mortified? Why, for heaven's sake?"

"I can't seem to stop this winning streak."

"Can't *stop* it!"

"Naturally—it's out of the question for me to make a profit on a venture of this sort. In my position. You can see that."

Miss Maxson picked up some of his chips. "Give us blues," she said to the croupier. "For the whole thing."

The trade was made. "You'll help me—play them in?" He seemed relieved.

"Professor, I'm going to get the money. This is your night. And it's your time to quit."

"But the money isn't mine!"

"It's as much yours as any money in this room is anybody's." They were attracting attention. She moved closer to him and whispered. "No fooling, Professor! Cash in the chips while you've got a lead! It's smart. The Club won't miss the money. I'm terribly glad you won. Please!"

Groggily, he picked up the chips and walked to the window. He was paid eight hundred and eighty-six dollars. When he put the bills in his wallet, his hands shook: it was by far the largest sum of money his wallet had ever contained. It was equal to two month's salary. Gambling money, criminal money, illicit gain—and he was accepting it because Miss Maxson insisted! Because, perhaps, he was accustomed to carrying out the orders of the opposite sex to the letter. It always saved trouble—he had learned that, long ago.

He looked up at Miss Maxson and she smiled.

He looked back at the table and the place where he had stood had been closed up. They had forgotten him already—taken his departure, with his winnings, as a simple matter of course. He could not think what he was going to do. Keep the matter secret—obviously. His whole evening's escapade had boomeranged!

"Buy me another drink?" She was still smiling.

"Of course!"

"We'll go back to the bar."

They did not, however, go back to the bar. They started—and that was all.

A man in the uniform of a police officer came suddenly from the corridor. He was not holding a gun, but he was wearing a large gun. Behind him were what seemed to the professor a platoon, at least, of police.

The man shouted, "All right—everybody! Stop the wheels! Hold those dice! This is a raid!"

There was silence. Then funny noises began. Women escaped. Men swore. Voices quickly rose up the scale. The place roared.

The police officer held up his hands and gestured at the sounds—as if they were tangible and could be pushed. "Listen, everybody! *Lissssen!* All we're taking is the wheels! Before any dame faints, or any damn fool guy tries to start anything—*lissen!* We're not hauling you in. We're not even taking names. Just keep out of our way while we get the wheels—and then you can go quietly. I don't want any arguments"—he stopped for a man who had hurried up to him—"and I don't give a hoot how important you are! This is a raid. The joint is closed!"

While this speech was being made, Professor Burke had been as aware of Miss Maxson as of the spectacular pandemonium. She had glanced—rather furtively—at her watch, when the police rushed in. It seemed an odd thing to do. Hysterical

33

reflex, no doubt. She had grown rather pale, after that. He supposed, since she was a hostess, that she was going to be arrested. The idea annoyed him.

But now, keeping her eyes on the police—who were already pushing one of the tables toward the corridor—she said softly, "Stay here and wait for me, will you?"

"Certainly."

She tapped on an inconspicuous door and was let into the cashier's booth. From there, she vanished.

He turned with interest to the scene around him. One or two of the ladies lolled in chairs and their escorts fanned them. Half a dozen of the gentlemen were in states of apoplectic rage. Professor Burke felt this was uncalled for: the law was Right— ergo wrath was wrong. They were gambling; they had earned this their discomfiture.

At the same time, he felt intensely gratified that names were not to be taken. He could imagine the attitude of the Dean—the President—the entire Faculty—if the morning papers disclosed that he had been seized in a raid on a gambling establishment! The thought brought perspiration on his brow.

A passing policeman noted it. "Pull yourself together, Bud," he said amiably.

Miss Maxson, meantime, had entered the office of the owner. Double-O was sitting on, not behind, his desk. His eyes were like flint.

The Tip was there, too—looking frightened.

Several other men—in tuxedos—stood about uneasily.

"They were an hour early," the girl said.

"Tell us something we don't know!" Chicago grated in The Tip's voice, this time.

Double-O Sanders looked toward her—his eyes seeming to see nothing. His lips moved. "It's a cross."

She swallowed.

His head turned slowly, so that his gaze was fixed on the safe. "They'll take all of us—and the operating dough—to Headquarters. I don't know who ordered this. But I do know they wanted to find the dough right here. They'll hold it for a cut. Maybe take it all." The faintest scorn sounded in his quiet words. "Legal confiscation."

The Tip said, "Let's split it and lam."

Double-O appeared not to have heard that. "All of us—except you, Connie." He turned toward her again. "Those cops know you?"

"I don't know any policemen." She smiled faintly. "Except one traffic cop named McGuire."

He handed the envelopes to her. "Get going."

"If they don't see me coming out of here."

He walked to the safe, after a moment. He masked it with his body and spun its dials. The door opened. "Envelopes," he said. "Plain, white. Large. Top left drawer."

The Tip hurriedly procured them. Double-O took three. Into two of them he put unopened packages of bills—into the third, a partly exhausted package. The girl saw the denominations. She grew paler.

He handed the envelopes to her. "Get going."

She took two books from a case behind his desk. She put the envelopes between the books. She wrinkled her nose at him and the door closed behind her.

The Tip said, "No kidding, Double-O! Adame . . . !"

Mr. Sanders raised his adze-blade eyes.

The Tip looked away.

There was a knock on the door opposite the one Miss Maxson had used.

"Come in, boys," Double-O called. "Not locked."

Miss Maxson approached the professor—through the crowd. Most of the tables had been pushed out of the room now. Their leg-marks showed in the deep carpets.

The officer looked in. "All right! Get going! We've taken the Club personnel—so you'll have to find your own cars in the yard. I've got a couple of men out there to unscramble you—but drive easy, and you won't get scrambled!"

The girl drew him deeper into the crowd. She handed him three hefty envelopes. "Keep these for me, will you?"

He thrust them into his jacket pockets—two on one side, one on the other. They showed. She started to protest—and changed her mind. Maybe it was better that way.

She dropped the books on the nearest chair. "Would you take me home? I have no car."

"I'd be delighted!"

It seemed very warm out of doors. The Club Egret was near the sea and the night air smelled salty. They walked around to the parking yard. Cars were starting—motors accelerated as if in anger, headlights snapping on. It was confusing. He finally found his repainted coupé. She got in. He started the motor. A slow, gear-gnashing, bumper-banging defile moved indignantly toward the street. He drove to Collins and turned south.

"I'm sorry about the raid," she said.

He looked at her buoyantly. "On my account? I wouldn't have missed it for anything! Though I regret winning. However! It was a risk I chose to take. I'm most grateful to you!"

"You don't owe me—or the Club—anything!" She said it in a peculiar tone. *If he knew what was in his pockets!* . . . He would never know— she thought.

"Where do you live?"

"On Di Lido Island. That's one of the Venetian Islands . . ."

"I know."

"The raid," she said, "was just window dressing. We ought to be open again in a day or two."

He was surprised. The car swerved a little—and he braked. He looked in his mirror to be sure he was not endangering traffic. "You mean those weren't police?"

"Oh—they were police, all right. What I mean is, we have raids early in the season and late in the season—before the big money arrives in Miami and after it goes—to satisfy the reform element." She explained the technique of the South Florida gambling raid—a gesture greatly satisfying to right-thinking citizens and of little hardship to casino operators.

Professor Burke listened while he turned right on Forty-First Street, went over the high, picturesque bridge and turned left on Pine Tree Drive.

Then he said, "I don't know whether it means anything or not, but there is a large sedan following us. It's been behind us ever since we started down Collins." He looked away, then, from the tunnel his headlights made between the Australian pines. She had not replied.

Miss Maxson appeared to be sick. She glanced back. She drew a couple of shaky breaths. She tried to light a cigarette—and used three matches.

And at last she said, very earnestly, "Gee, Professor, I'm sorry I got you in this one! Those are —hijackers."

Five:

MOST MEN who found themselves in Professor Burke's situation would have been alarmed. Miami Beach, through the center of which he was driving, advertises to the world its attractions and its distractions. It is more quiet about its civic detractions. Not the least of these is the boldness and the frequency of its robberies. Holdups of bejeweled, home-bound revelers, burglaries, and daylight stick-ups of cash-carrying citizens are almost a part of the local climate.

It was of this that Professor Burke somewhat anxiously thought. "Don't be so perturbed," he said. "At the end of this street is a fire station. Suppose I simply turn in there?"

"That would be the last thing to do! Although—"

"I suppose," he mused, glancing at his mirror, "they saw me make that big haul—and followed us . . ."

She said something. He murmured, "I beg your pardon?"

"I just swore, that was all. Don't you realize *why* we're being followed? The envelopes—the ones I gave you!"

39

He touched a pocket. "Those letters?"

"Letters! Ye gods, Professor! *Letters!* The police staged the raid an hour early. Surprised us. They were after the operating capital of the Club Egret . . ."

The car lurched a little. "You mean to say—in those envelopes—?"

"—are two unopened packets of thousands, and one partly gone. Something like two hundred and sixty or seventy thousand dollars. Look out! You'll ram a tree!"

His voice squeaked. "You mean to say I've got a quarter of a million dollars right here in my pockets?"

"I mean you have."

"Then who . . . ?" he glanced at the mirror again—and now he was afraid. Chillingly afraid.

The girl said, "If you turn in, the firemen will call the cops—and they'll get it, after all."

"Corrupt police," he murmured bitterly.

"Corrupt police, nothing! They were just carrying out orders. It's somebody bigger than cops, who would get that money—or a piece of it."

For a moment, he merely drove. He had started at a careful thirty. He had notched it up to thirty-five, from nervousness. He dropped back, as self-discipline.

"The car behind us," she went on, after a pause, *"could* be a lot of people. But it is most likely somebody who knew the police were going to spring their raid early in order to snatch Double-O's money. And that, most likely, would mean the Maroon Gang. Have you ever heard of them?"

"Yes, I have," he said jerkily. "There's an excellent monograph by Longreve and Bilchard on the Maroon Gang. Organized in the prohibition era by a man named—"

"Never mind the lecture! If that's who it is— and if they think we have the money—which they must—we'll be lucky if we're alive tomorrow morning."

He turned into Dade Boulevard—the tranquil canal on one side, the empty, night-hung golf course on the other. He cast a reluctant glance at the fire station.

Thought, he kept assuring himself, was imperative. The men in the following car were—by his own definition—virtually incapable of thought. He found, however, that thinking was difficult, under these circumstances.

For one thing, he could not drive up to the nearest police station, like any ordinary citizen in distress. That would mean some sort of infamous "confiscation" of the funds now in their care. Illegal funds, to be sure, but Professor Burke disliked to surrender a quarter of a million dollars either to hostile gangsters or corrupt politicians.

He drove out onto the first of the many bridges which connect the Venetian Islands with Miami and Miami Beach.

"What are you going to do?" she asked.

"Think," he said.

41

"It's too late! My house isn't far ahead. If we go there, they'll get us there. If we go on, they'll stop us—probably in the dark stretch where the street divides."

Up ahead, at the side of the road, a red eye gleamed. A siren growled.

Instinctively, he slowed. There were signals to show that one of the two drawbridges on the causeway was about to be raised. With the tail of his eye, he caught sight of a moonlight excursion boat moving toward the span.

The girl said, "Step on it!"

He did so—as he saw what she meant.

The bridge siren growled loudly. He perceived that they would get under the first gate. He heard a bellow from the bridge tender. Their wheels hummed on the steel lattice of the lift-spans. The far gate ticked the top of the car. The headlights of the pursuing sedan wobbled as brakes stopped it. The bridge tender blew a whistle. But they were going fast. Across Rivo Alto Island—across more bridges—and onto Di Lido. The car behind them was held up.

He stopped—under a street light.

The girl moaned. "Keep *going!* We might duck them in Miami! We've got a couple of minutes, anyhow!"

The professor spoke tersely. "In the glove compartment! Postage stamps! When I put them in my pockets, they stick together in this steamy climate. When I put them in the compartment, I forget them." He had taken out his fountain pen. He also took out his wallet. He transferred its contents into the least bulky envelope. "This Mr. Double-O Sanders' address?"

She had opened the compartment. "He lives at the Bombay Royale Hotel on Collins Avenue." At their side, she saw the green, metal mailbox. It was for this—not light—that he had stopped. He was already scribbling.

He handed one to her and she licked it. She pressed firmly, with a shaky hand. "It's pretty heavy . . ."

"Stick a lot of stamps on it! You'll find fifty threes, there."

She tore, and stuck on, a lot. The next was ready. Then the third. She ran with them to the box and hurried back to the car. He let in the clutch.

"Turn right at the next corner. *What* an idea!"

He drove two blocks. They could hear the siren purr as the bridge opened. She pointed out a large house, looming whitely among still larger trees. A wall surrounded it—a white wall with an iron gate.

He swung the car around and parked on the grass, under the thick limbs of a sea grape. He left his lights on, purposely. "Do they know you live here?"

"If it's anybody from the Maroon Gang, probably."

"Then, listen," he said. "They don't know me.

43

We've driven very slowly—and rather erratically —all the way. If they know you live at this address, they will probably drive by here. We will have had very little time to dispose of a large sum of money. For all they can be sure of, we may never have had the money. Our drive together may have had a—romantic—rather than a commercial— reason. If we were now to give that possibility some verisimilitude . . ."

In the dashboard light, her handsome eyes flickered a little. Her hands went to her hair and did something. It tumbled around her shoulders like suddenly sickled wheat. She wiped her lips on a small handkerchief and dropped it. "Might as well look as if we'd prepared for it," she said.

Then she kissed him.

It was necessary to get the right amount of lipstick—not too much, but enough—in the right places, she thought.

Cars began moving on the Venetian Way, two blocks below. One slowed, and turned. It was the large, dark sedan. It picked up speed—evidently as their lights were observed.

"You better have your arms around me," she said.

"Do you always—kiss people that way?"

The sedan crossed to the wrong side of the road, and stopped, bumper touching bumper. Five men got out, fast. They had handkerchiefs tied under their eyes. All of them held guns. One—

the fattest—said, "Out, Miss Maxson, please. Out, whoever you are, if you please. Be quick!"

The professor spoke indignantly. "Really, I haven't a dime. Well—a dime, perhaps. Some change. My bills—frittered away at the club. The young lady—"

"Out!" said the fat man.

Professor Burke got out. He was swiftly searched.

"You will stand between our car and the wall. If a car comes on this street, kneel. If you yell—zut!"

The accent was French. But what kind of French? Belgian? The Professor waited for more words, as he and the girl moved between the wall and the big, black car.

"Now, Miss Maxson. Where is the money?"

"What money?"

The fat man with the accent slapped her face.

Professor Burke had never before seen such a thing. He walked up to the Frenchman. "See here, my good man. More brutality of that sort and I shall either compel you to shoot me or make mince meat of you. Violence is intolerable. Violence to a lady is beyond countenancing."

There was a long silence. Finally the fat leader said, "Just who are you?"

"Professor Burke, the socio-psychologist."

There was more thought. "Who is La Cavour, then?"

45

The "ou" sound was Germanic. *Alsatian,* the Professor suddenly felt sure. "Phillippe La Cavour is a second-rate French criminal psychologist, born in Lyon, and guilty of some atrociously superficial hypothesizing—"

"What, precisely, are you doing here?"

"Isn't it rather painfully obvious?"

The fat man turned. "Miss Maxson, you were the only one in Double-O's club not on the list to be taken to Headquarters. I assumed you would have the club's valuables."

"You assumed a lot."

The masked face turned farther. "The car—boys! Upholstery and all. A couple of you make sure they didn't toss it over the wall."

Time passed.

Professor Burke tried to back up far enough to see the license number. A wobble of the gun and a soft, "Ah, no!" stopped him. He looked the car over, trying to fix the details in his mind. He was not very good at the years of cars. The wheels showed traces of a white mark which makes sticky ruts on certain minor roads in South Florida. Some vegetation was caught in one of the door hinges. By leaning against the car and clinging to that hinge, he was able to remove a sample of the vegetation. Hedge or driveway shrubbery, he thought. He shifted his position and put it in his pocket.

The sound of upholstery being rent by a knife came from the coupé. Rustlings were heard as two of the men inspected the ground under the shrubbery behind the wall. A car approached. The knelt. The men ripping up the coupé put out their flashlights and sat down. The car swept on.

Eventually, the fat man sighed. "I could, of course, have made an incorrect guess."

"Several," the Professor said emphatically. The Frenchman ignored that. "Naturally, I regret the damage to your car. You seem, however, to be a man fond of unusual risk." He looked thoughtfully at the girl. "So you will not mind this comparatively trifling misfortune. Good night, Professor."

"Bon soir," the professor said, *"Mauvais rêves."*

The four men had given up. Their leader beckoned with his gun. They climbed into the sedan. Their car could be heard on the now-silent causeway as it gathered speed.

"Come in," the girl said, after they stopped listening. "I'll make you some coffee."

"Thanks, but I think not. Bedelia will be worried."

"Bedelia? The little woman?"

"My landlady," he said in an injured tone.

She kissed him suddenly. "Thanks. See you." The gate banged behind her.

It was uncomfortable, driving on the hacked upholstery, with bare springs protruding here and there.

Six:

MEN WHO receive their early, ethical training from a woman and who, as a result, respond automatically to feminine suggestion, are inclined to resent the fact and to feel dominated. Professor Burke could not repress a sensation of almost childish glee as he drove up to Bedelia's home.

The night was still, the stars were wan but numerous, and the air was sweet with the various flowers that had accumulated around Bedelia's house from years of trading among garden club members. A light glowed in her living room— like the light that burns in windows for sailors. When his wheels touched the drive, a light came on in the car porte. Bedelia appeared, enormous, anxious, and swathed in decorous kimono.

"Good heavens, Martin, it's nearly two o'clock!"

He stepped out of the car. She saw the lipstick and followed it here and there on his composed features. Then she saw the ripped upholstery.

"Mercy!" she gasped. "What was she—a tigress?"

Over a pot of coffee, he told her the story. He omitted, however, his first reactions to Miss Maxson and his later sensations when she had kissed him. There were, beyond doubt, the most important elements.

"So—as you can see—" he summed up, "the whole fantastic affair demonstrated that mere intelligence is sufficient to deal even with criminals of the stature of that fat Alsatian."

"Plus a lucky break in the matter of a drawbridge . . ."

"I include that. The causeway drawbridges are constantly being raised for passing boats. Quite frequently, even at night. But here—also—it was a matter of intelligence. Miss Maxson's. She simply capitalized on an opportunity."

"And if the bridge hadn't gone up?"

"We would doubtless have contrived other measures."

She poured more coffee and stared at him. "Martin, do you realize that you carried your life in your hands? For such a sum—for a fraction of it—a gang like that would have murdered you both without a scruple!"

"Possibly." He glimmered his eyes at her. "But 'all's well that ends well.' I shall be able to make the experience into a separate lecture. I have here materials to demonstrate the essential stupidity of the criminal, the superiority of the resourceful mind, and the futility of such imbecile pastimes as gambling."

"But it wasn't! You won eight hundred dollars!"

"Not 'won,' Bedelia. Dishonorably accumulated. And it's gone."

"You mean—you don't expect to get it back?"

"Certainly not! Double-O Sanders is, after all,

49

a gambler. I enclosed my winnings—and the balance of the money I had from you—simply because I hated it to fall into the hands of whoever operated the following car."

And you aren't going back to the Club Egret?"

"Whatever for?"

She slowly shook her head. There were times when what he regarded as clear thinking, or proper behavior, seemed obtuse to her—and more than obtuse: downright dumb.

The morning was clear and rather cool: towards dawn, a very slight high pressure front moved in from the northwest. People had wood fires going on their hearths and in iron stoves. These sent over the inhabited rim of the peninsula a drift of pine smoke which carried far out to sea. Inland, the pungent aroma drifted over the campus of the University, about which there was a definite vacation motif.

Professor Burke conducted his last two recitation classes with unusual vivacity. His students, being themselves in good spirit, attributed it to the same cause: imminence of the holidays. Had they known that on the previous night he had defied and successfully outsmarted five members of the Maroon Gang, with the aid of a blonde who looked not unlike a movie star, they would have been flabbergasted beyond precedent.

They had, of course, no such knowledge. He

intended to divulge it months later—when he was thoroughly detached from it. A professor could mention gambling "last year" with decorum. "Last night" was far too recent.

At noon, he finished his seminar on freshman socio-psychology and started across the footpath through the Bermuda grass to the College Inn Tearoom. Here, he encountered Miss Marigold Macey—because she had been waiting for him.

"Hello," she said. "I wanted to ask you a couple of questions." This was a mild deceit for he was meant to presume the questions referred to his science.

He said, "I was just about to have lunch. Perhaps . . . ?"

"That would be divine!"

Professor Burke did not, as a rule, dine with students. Their "gay banter" seemed, to him, insufferable twaddle. Miss Macey, being somewhat older, might be looked upon as an exception.

The tearoom smelled like the hot raisins in its infinitudes of muffins—a large chamber with oak pillars where the waitresses were semicostumed in starched, colored aprons. They found, luckily, a table for two.

Miss Macey had seen to it that her curly-casual hair-do was in proper condition, her lipstick was on straight, and her white sandals were immaculate. As she had said to Wally Stratton, she was not an extroverted Southern belle. Thus she was not able to sit on his desk casually—pat his hand, hold his arm, call him "honey" in a becloyed manner, bat her eyes at him, or switch herself about. The circumstances did not leave her without certain resources.

After they had ordered lunch, she looked up at him with a polka tempo in her large, brown eyes. "I'm getting a great deal out of your course, Professor Burke."

"I'm delighted!"

"I really wanted to apologize for being so impertinent, yesterday. I wish I hadn't been."

If she only knew! he thought. He beamed at her. "Argument is the staircase on which knowledge climbs." It sounded fuddy-duddyish. He wondered what fuddy-duddy had said it—and realized he had coined the maxim himself! "You know," he said, in a less sententious tone, "it's very dull when there isn't any—criticism or resistance. You get the feeling that you're not really teaching anybody anything. Just setting up echoes from sources that won't retain the sound at all."

"I never thought of that. It must be discouraging." She returned to her "impertinence." "What I did yesterday was very unfair. Nobody in his right mind expects a professor to do the sorts of things he presents in theory."

He found himself trembling, slightly. Miss Macey possessed the power to affect him. And what she had just said supplied a perfect opening for an exchange of such affects. He ate a forkful of creamed chipped beef. "As a matter of fact,"

52

he finally said, "and in the strictest confidence, I—understated the case yesterday. I wouldn't want it to get beyond you—"

Her lips were parted. The expression in her eyes now was entirely uncontrived. "Of course not!"

"—but I've had a good deal more—ah—vivid experience with the world of crime—with gangsters, gambling, and so on—than most people."

"No! You—Professor?"

He raised one shoulder and let it fall. "I've won—and lost—" he added hurriedly, "at roulette. Not—recently, of course. I've seen gunplay—"

"Gunplay! Where?"

He was unsure that the use of firearms merely for hold-up constituted "gunplay" in the technical sense. He hastened away from the subject. "One or two of the nation's foremost criminals know me. At least one is somewhat beholden to me."

"Why—that's the most wonderful ever!"

He frowned. "Wonderful?" He was beginning to feel that he had overstepped. But the effect on Miss Macey was a pleasing radiance. The brevity of his sleep on the previous night had, no doubt, made him slightly toxic—and the toxins had perhaps produced a lightheadedness.

"Wonderful—of course," she said. "But you know"—her eyes were disturbingly bright—"I think I sort of suspected it. I had a hunch that inside—underneath—you were entirely different."

53

"No man," he replied, "keeps all the cards of his personality face up." He felt the figure was particularly apt. "No man—and especially, no professor."

"Couldn't you come over to my house, sometime? Dad and Mother would love to meet you. I've often talked to them about you. Or—wouldn't it be fair for me to get an extracurricular education from you?"

Extracurricular education. It was an interesting phrase. "I'm afraid—from what I've heard—that I'd have to fight my way through a swarm of male undergraduates."

Miss Macey laughed—and stopped laughing. She said gently, "You wouldn't have to fight at all, Professor."

That did it.

Women seldom acknowledge the fact; more often, they repress it vigorously; but the fact remains, as all men know: there is a certain contagion in romance, at least among males. The man who breaks down and kisses Girl A is more liable to kiss Girl B than the man who held himself aloof from A.

What was happening to the Professor was a variant of that phenomenon. He was looking at Miss Macey—thinking about Miss Maxson. He recalled, with the utmost clearness of detail, his sensations at the time of her kiss. Or kisses. He perceived that the same sensation—or possibly a different and even more powerful one—could be produced by, or elicited from, another: Marigold Macey. It is a shattering experience. He stared at the girl in a way which, he reasoned afterward, must have been appalling. She merely blushed a little and looked away. He decided to ask her when he might see her at home.

A hand pounded his back. "Wellll—Burke!"

The trancelike mood collapsed. He turned. Feebly, he said, "Ah. MacFalkland."

"What are you doing—flirting with my gold partner?" He saw surprise. "Yeah! She and young Stratton and Mrs. Ames have a foursome this afternoon, old boy. Hi, Marigold!"

"Oh, I see. Very pleasant."

"You ought to get out more, Burke," MacFalkland said. "Rode by your lecture hall yesterday. Heard you droning away. Well—see you by and by, Marigold!"

He strode away, waving heartily at people here and there in the room. Professor Burke sagged. MacFalkland was, after all, a natural leader—the sort of man who should head up a department.

"He's a friend of Daddy's," Miss Macey said uncomfortably. "Daddy's a judge, you know."

"I didn't."

"Yes. Mac—Professor MacFalkland—works with Daddy on several things. Slum clearance projects."

The luncheon regressed into a rather ordinary professor-student meal.

Seven:

HIS SCHEDULE wound up, that day, at four. He walked home, reflecting on the range of moods which accompanied any regular route, such as his. Item one, Miss Macey. He could see her happily married to such a chap as that ex-pilot, Stratton. Item two. MacFalkland. When the University could afford a full-scale Socio-Psychology Department, MacFalkland would be the director. He, Burke, would live in the imminence of that boisterous voice and sudden back-slap. The third item was more difficult to define: a vague, almost sad sense that a bright light had winked in his life—and gone out.

Bedelia called from the side porch. "Want tea?"

He came around the house.

"Your car's been hauled to the garage. The man estimated it would cost around a hundred dollars."

"Gosh." He munched a bit of orange cake.

"I sponged your dinner clothes. With alcohol—for the lipstick. And sent them to the cleaner this morning."

"Thank you, Bedelia."

56

"There were pieces of fern in the pocket."

"Fern? In the pocket?"

"I didn't know what it was, either. I took it to Alice Beardsley. She's secretary of the garden club."

"However—oh!" He smiled faintly. "Last night. I really was dramatizing myself, Bedelia. Looking for clues. Observing closely. All sorts of idiocy. That wad of plant stuff came from the hinge of the sedan that held us up."

"It did?" she leaned forward interestedly.

"What of it? Hedge somewhere."

"It only grows on certain Keys. A subspecies. The fronds are much wilder on one side than the other."

"You don't say!"

"Which means, of course, that car last night had very recently made a trip to the Keys."

"Marl."

"What?"

"I said 'marl.' There was whitish marl on the tires and wheels. The kind you see in ruts on those little sides roads in the Keys."

"That proves it! Alice gave me a list of the Keys where the fern is known to grow. Only four or five. We could drive down Sunday . . ."

"Drive down? What on earth for?"

"Aren't you curious? Wouldn't you like to know just *what* a carload of gangsters were doing in the Keys? And *where* they did it?"

"Heavens, no! Why should I? Fishing trip,

perhaps. Maybe they own a juke joint down there. What of it?"

"I would be mighty curious." She settled back. "Do you remember the tires?"

"Diamonds and dots," he said. "Alternating. But I'm not going on any wild-goose chase in the Keys. I'm going to finish up the marks for the month, and eat dinner, and read Conover's *Hidden Social Culprits*—and get a good night's sleep. I'm tired out."

He was not too tired to hurry down the stairs when, at six, she called him to the phone. There was something in Bedelia's voice.

"Hello?"

"Hello, darling!"

His reaction was like near-electrocution—short of fatal, but violent. "Miss—Maxson!"

Bedelia put the lid on the veal curry, quietly.

"I wheedled your number out of the University operator. What you doing this evening?"

"Well—I was—that is—"

"I'll pick you up around eight-thirty—after supper . . ."

This time, he made it more effectual. "I really couldn't, Miss Maxson. I've got work to do. And—my dinner things—"

"The hell with your dinner things! Wear shorts, if you feel like it. A certain person wants to meet you."

He opened his mouth to say it was utterly out of the question. But the light had winked on again.

58

And it was not his doing. He gave her the address.

Bedelia was elated. "You know, Martin, girls aren't any different now, from my time. They simply go out and act the way we merely used to feel."

"I have no business letting her do it."

"You have no business missing such an opportunity! Even if only for my sake—so I can get a look at her. I'll be at the window curtain, sure as shooting!"

Eight:

MISS CONSTANCE MAXSON drove up quietly, walked through the lush front yard, and knocked on the door. Bedelia answered, and called up the stairs for the professor. He came—rather nervously. "You've met?"

Connie nodded and Bedelia boomed, "Prettiest girl this house has seen in ages!"

The car at the curb was a convertible, long and grey and brand new. Connie drove toward Miami. She seemed to be serenely pleased with the world—and not inclined to talk.

"What happened?" he finally asked, breaking through their occasional amiable platitudes.

"Double-O will tell you. How do you like this car?"

"It's a beauty."

"It's yours."

He gasped. "Mine!"

"From Double-O. In repayment for your coupé!"

"I couldn't accept it! It's—fabulously magnanimous. But I couldn't think of such a thing!"

Connie smiled. "I told him you'd refuse it. You know, Professor, you're something of a sweet-

60

heart." After a while she said, "I suspect that Double-O may be a shock to you. You better get set."

"I'm quite prepared to meet him on his own terms."

Connie turned over the new grey convertible to the doorman of the Bombay Royale, whisked the professor through the lobby so fast he only glimpsed the photomurals of Hindu temples, and took him to the roof in a private elevator. On the roof he could taste the sea and hear a rumba band playing in the patio far below. The girl knocked at the door of a small penthouse; it was opened by a butler.

"Come in, Miss Maxson. Professor Burke, good evening," the butler said.

The professor experienced a series of stupefactions. The room behind the butler was furnished with modern pieces and a few Eighteenth Century French chairs. A fire was burning on a marble hearth. There was a white cat curled under the piano. On the walls were etchings of cats by Peggy Bacon and a magnificent print of a Cézanne.

A man rose from a chair which was set in front of corner bookcases, beside a lamp and a small table. He turned a book face down. This he did slowly, unhinging his long frame—and smiling. The book was Professor Burke's own *Ruminations of a Socio-Psychologist*.

"Very kind of you to come over," Double-O said. "I should really have called on you. I've been

61

reading your collected lectures. Most interesting. Before the evening's over, perhaps I could add a few bits to your theory of crime. It was theoretical interest that brought you to the Egret last night, my niece says."

His eyes were twinkling. He held out his hand.

Professor Burke looked at Connie in a sort of frenzy. "Niece?"

The tall, lanky gambler said, "Oh-oh!" He cocked an eyebrow at the girl and then at the professor. "Who did she say she was?"

"I told him," Connie answered, giggling, "that I was a hostess. It's true enough. I think he assumed I was your moll, Bill. So I let him think so—for punishment."

The professor was scarlet. "I honestly—as a matter of fact—the truth is—I made no estimate."

Double-O walked to the grate to hide his grin. He poked the fire. "Women," he said, "are cads, Professor. Born bounders. Connie's mother is my half sister, and hardly proud of the fact. I'm the family black sheep. Connie herself, however, has a drop of the restless Sanders blood. This year —since no polite institution for young ladies could hold her—I hired her to keep people happy at the Egret."

"I supervise the kitchen," Connie said proudly. "And I helped re-do the gambling room. Isn't it gorgeous?"

"Very," said the professor—that being as much as he could say for the moment. Fortunately for him, the butler wheeled in a tea wagon and Double-O mixed a Tom Collins for Connie and a Scotch and water for the professor. For himself he made nothing, and explained that he did not drink.

"Now," he said, taking the chair in which he had been sitting, "I would enjoy the story from you, Professor Burke."

"First," the professor said, "I'd like to know—how things turned out?"

Double-O laughed. "They kept all of us at Headquarters till morning. They searched the place—ripped it up a bit. Let us go finally. I called Connie—"

The girl had taken a seat on the floor by the fire and the cat was in her lap. "I asked him to look at his mail."

The gambler went to a desk and took an envelope from the drawer. "Your money, Professor. Connie says part of it represents winnings at my tables. I'm delighted!"

"In other words—the—funds—reached you?"

"Yes, Professor. They did. Thanks to you. Now —let's have the story."

Professor Burke told it, in bare outline and with several deletions. Double-O listened—his face reflecting understanding, excitement, appreciation. "I suppose," he said when the professor finished, "that you knew French Paul would just as soon use a gun as not?"

"He slapped Miss Maxson—with no need. She hadn't even refused to answer his query. He simply

63

slapped her. Brutally. There was no alternative for me but to tell the swine—"

"No alternative, eh?" Double-O's grey eyes seemed amused. "I also suppose you realize you quite possibly saved a very large sum of my money from confiscation? Not to mention my niece's life—perhaps—if she'd been alone."

"He wouldn't accept the car—" Connie said.

Double-O nodded. "I was afraid of that." He stretched his legs and looked at his shoes for a moment. "Professor," he said, "I'm possibly a curious man—from your viewpoint. My ideas of ethics may differ from your ideas. But I think our concept of gratitude must be about the same. I never owed any one so much as I owe you. It was foolish to offer the car and hope you'd accept. I realize I haven't anything you would accept. One trifle, perhaps—the hospitality of the Club Egret. If you will be our regular guest for dinner this winter—with your friends—I'll be happy. I'll be disappointed if you won't. The Club is yours. And if I could think of anything else . . ."

To his astonishment, Professor Burke found himself very much moved. He momentarily felt that tears might come in his eyes, which would have been a hideous embarrassment. He had looked forward to meeting the notorious Double-O as a source of firsthand—and scornful—lecture material. But the man in front of him—obviously cultured, plainly sincere—was very upsetting.

The professor's eyes moved away—and fastened

on the Cézanne. It was not, he realized, a print. It was real.

"I told you," Connie said softly to her uncle, "the guy was nice."

Double-O nodded very slightly at her. His grey eyes followed the professor's. "Like it? I do. One of my—clients—lost quite a large sum of money. He happened to be pressed for cash at the moment and offered the painting." The cat walked over and the gambler stroked it absently.

Professor Burke's mind finally churned through his emotions and the surprises which had given rise to them. Somehow, he felt, he had been guilty of an indecency. Intuition led him to say what he did. "Mr. Sanders, I'll be glad to be your guest some evening. I'd like Bedelia—my landlady, and a unique character—to see the Club Egret. But there *is* one thing you can do for me."

The barest trace of surprise showed in the gambler's face. It was followed by a smile. "Name it!"

"For years," the professor said quietly, "I've postured as an authority on—on—"

"—the way the other half lives?"

"Exactly. But the fact is, I'm an ignoramus. My information is thirdhand—fourthhand—theoretical . . ."

The gambler looked at the face-down book and hid the ghostly beginning of a smile. "On the contrary. I thought—"

"No college professor has had an opportunity

for a—a briefing, by anyone who really knows the story. If you could understand the difficulty of discussing a subject without firsthand knowledge . . ."

Double-O nodded. He walked over and again poked up the fire. "We'll start, Professor, with the gents you met last night. French Paul—who's the present chief of the Maroon Gang—"

"An Alsatian."

The gambler turned his head and smiled. "You're quick. Yes. Born in Strasbourg, actually. The Maroon Gang began moving in on Greater Miami several years ago. I once ran their gambling—in three cities. We had a disagreement about—ethics. I'll tell you their political set-up here. It's as good an example as any. Their interests in Miami, at first, were bookmaking, a few protection rackets, and the usual other enterprises. I gather from word that gets around that lately they've branched into the business of bringing in aliens who shouldn't be here. Former Nazis who got out with loot. Possibly a few well-heeled people working for Russia. After all, Florida is full of tricky back doors to the U.S.—the rivers that run into the Everglades—the Ten Thousand Islands— the Keys . . ."

Professor Burke concealed a sudden, internal start. *Marl and fern,* he thought. He hadn't mentioned these matters, in his account of the pursuit and holdup: his sleuthing impulse had seemed childish.

Double-O went on. "Whatever makes money, interests the Maroon Gang. I'll tell you how they muscled in here—and how they got set. I didn't believe, until last night, that they were going to work me over. What happened makes it plain they have a better setup than mine. They know the whole score. They intended to beat the cops at a snatch of my working capital. I've banked it now, incidentally. Even my own club isn't safe any longer. However. When I sketch the background on the Maroons—who they are— how they operate—where they come from—how they got that way—you'll know as much as I do about all of the gangs. I'm a gambler, Professor. Never had another angle. If I get pushed out of business, I'll go. My connections are sound, so it will take a lot of pushing. After I tell you about the Maroon Gang, I'll tell you the long and not always dull story of my own life. How I grew up. Why I quit college. Where I learned—my profession. Is that what you want?"

"I'd like to hear it myself," Connie said.

Double-O lighted a cigar, and smoked for a minute. "What you are going to learn, Professor, you never heard. I never told you. If you use it as a background for lectures—or books—or anything—it'll just be your surmises and bald assertions. Every big shot in the rackets and every involved politician will deny it. Will that suit your purposes?"

"Yes," the professor said. "And more than repay any debt you may feel in my direction."

It was after one o'clock when Connie accompanied him to the lobby.

He said, bemusedly, "I'll get a cab . . ."

"I'll drive you over."

"Not at this hour—with the long ride back. I refuse!"

"Will we—I—see you again, Professor?"

"Absolutely."

The doorman brought her car. They stood on the broad hotel steps. Already, the northwest high was diminishing. The warm winds of the Gulf Stream were pushing back over the immense, flat peninsula. Connie turned from her car—the one intended for him. She kissed him. "So long, Martin."

He was scarcely conscious of the ride in the cab. The amount of the meter shocked him. Then he remembered his winnings, paid, and tipped liberally. The driver thanked him and the red taillight of his cab whisked away on West Cortez Circle.

Bedelia was waiting up—naturally. The glass coffeemaker was full, and hot.

"You've got lipstick again," she said. "But not so much. She was a very nice girl. So much more refined than I'd expected. What *else* do you know?"

"Ask me what I don't know—it would be the shorter part." He sighed then, and sat down

68

tiredly at the kitchen table. "One thing, to start with. We're going to go down in the Keys and try to locate that fern subspecies, next Sunday. Bedelia!"—he shook his head—"you have no idea —no *idea*—of the way this world runs! And there are one or two things I mean to stop right now— or perish in the attempt! You're game, aren't you?"

For a few seconds, she had an odd, almost premonitory feeling. A feeling of violence, horror and sudden death. The kitchen seemed unfamiliar and she found herself thinking of the Keys—not in the brilliant light of day, but at night, with the sea quiet and ominously listening. She had launched the professor's little escapade. It was turning into—*what?* The feeling passed.

"You bet!" Bedelia replied.

Nine:

FEW PASTIMES are more innocent than amateur botany. Few persons, as a class, are more innocent than professors and the elderly widows of Naval officers. A less innocent pair of plant hunters than Professor Burke and Bedelia Ogilvy in all probability never existed. What they undertook to do, on a warm and sunny Sunday, was to verify the idea that certain members of the Maroon Gang had been smuggling aliens into the United States, by way of the Florida Keys.

The T-Men knew that an organization of some sort had been bringing notorious aliens into the country, by way of Canada, Mexico, or the seacoast. Two T-Men had been shot to death in a widespread attempt to add to this information—information which, such as it was, had been shared with F.B.I. and the Coast Guard.

Bedelia and Professor Burke had no notion of such facts. If they had been less ardent and more sophisticated—and particularly if he had not clung to his theory of the essential stupidity of criminals—they would have reported their suspicions to the police and let it go at that.

"What we know," he said chattily, as he drove

his reupholstered coupé onto the first of the Keys-connecting bridges, "is, basically, that a car belonging to the Maroon Gang had marl on its wheels—"

"—and had some ferns caught in its hinges that Alice Beardsley says grows only on DeWitt Key, Little Tango, Key Dent, and Lower Beacon Key." Bedelia was fully prepared for the adventure. She was wearing riding breeches and boots, and carrying a bee-hat, in case the insects became unbearable. She went on enthusiastically, "We have Mr. Sanders' hint that these Maroon people are engaged in the—business—"

"—and I will be able to recognize the tire-marks of that big sedan, if we find them. In marl of that sort, with no rains since, they should be very plain."

It was little enough to go on, in a sense. Little enough, but the multitudes of officials searching for the smugglers would have given much to know that little. It was for such small facts that they searched coast and border.

They drove to Lower Beacon Key, as a starting place. It was farthest from Miami, and the smallest of the four. They reached it before noon—an islet of twenty or thirty acres, without a tree. The ferns with the lopsided fronds covered about half of it. There was not a byroad on it—nothing but the main highway with its crescendo-diminuendo of Sunday traffic.

"We can rule this out immediately," Bedelia

said with assurance. "No cover. No lane. No wharf. Nothing. A swimmer wouldn't try to smuggle pearls ashore here."

Key Dent was bigger, and wooded. After lunch, they explored. There were three side roads on Key Dent. Two led to fishing camps, over dry coral. One led to a lobsterman's cabin, through a certain amount of damp, whitish marl. But there were no tire tracks of any sort in the marl.

They returned to their car. With no diminution of enthusiasm, they drove back to Little Tango which was the largest of the suspect four, in spite of its name. It boasted of a half-dozen homes, another fishing camp, and a combination filling station and marine curio store. There were many side roads and they spent the best part of the afternoon exploring them—without success. Some were a few hundred feet in length and some were several hundred yards. None even passed through the lopsided ferns, although many were rutted deeply in marl.

Before they continued on to DeWitt Key, the professor decided to fill up his gasoline tank. He drove in at the single pump of the filling station and curio shop. He blew his horn. An old man with a limp, a quid of tobacco, faded trousers and no shoes finally appeared and began to crank the gasoline by hand.

Bedelia liked shells and corals. She got out to inspect the collection in the shop. She returned disdainfully.

"Just junk," she said, "and most of it broken up. Poorly collected. But"—and she lowered her voice—"there's a road on the other side of the building that goes to a ramshackle garage—and also beyond it, toward the sea."

Professor Burke paid. "Do you mind," he enquired mildly, "if we go down your road? We're fern collectors—"

"Private property," the old man said.

"I realize that. I'd be glad to pay a dollar or two, however. We are hunting for a particular fern. It has been reported on four keys, only. This is one."

"It is lopsided," Bedelia said brightly. "I hope you won't object to our just looking."

"Sure do! Anyhow—place is full of mosquitoes—

"We're accustomed to that!" Bedelia popped the bee-hat over her head.

The old man was startled. He spat.

"Come, Martin," she said, "I'm certain he won't mind if we just take a peep. It would be a pity to leave Little Tango without finding the fern."

"Lady, I said this was private property."

Bedelia's head loomed from the open car door—bee-hat and all. It was quite a sight. "You sound," she said reprovingly, "as if you had something to hide back there. Have you, my good man? An alcohol still, or some such nuisance? I shall report that you have a still. I'm convinced you do have! Martin! We will stop at the office of the Peace Justice. Better still—when we get to Miami—"

73

"Lady," said the old man resignedly, "there is no still back there. No nothing. There is a dock where my son keeps his fishboat. He's outside fishing now. For Lord's sake, go back and see the danged ferns!"

The professor drove past the dilapidated garage and proceeded beneath the locked branches of trees toward a spot of water shining at the end of the long, green tunnel. Inside her bee-hat, Bedelia was chuckling.

Presently she said, "There are the danged ferns."

"And the marl!"

They got out. The ruts in the road were deep. They showed signs of frequent use. He bent over. The alternating diamonds and dots of automobile tires were plainly embossed here in the earth. "This is it," he murmured.

They walked toward the water, mosquitoes rising about them. The trees thinned and the ferns began. They were perhaps four feet in height, and the fronds of dozens had been broken off by whatever had passed on the road.

The water off the end of the wharf beyond was disappointingly shallow. Two feet, perhaps—weed beds and sand shoals. Sunblanched tree limbs marked what was not so much a channel as the shallow approach from the light blue sea over the distant reef and the far, purple line of the Gulf Stream. A lazy chop splashed on the low, white claylike shore. The lighthouse was a distant, dim finger. No boats were in view—nothing save the flat prospect of the ocean and the cloud-patterned sky. The dock foundation had been in place for a long time. But its jerry-made decking was nailed on two-by-eights and could be hauled inland at the prospect of rough weather.

The old man limped out on the wharf behind them. Professor Burke noticed the sag of his right suspender and the bulge in his pants pocket. "Find the still?" he chuckled.

"We found the ferns," Bedelia answered. "And small thanks to you!"

"Don't like snoopy people."

"No more do I like tobacco-chewing old gaffers!"

There was a clearing where a vehicle could be turned. Professor Burke spun his wheels in the deepest, slipperiest hole. Then they were on the road—the insects left behind.

Bedelia removed the bee-hat. "Now what?"

"Honestly, I don't know. I don't believe I really expected we'd find anything. However, we have found quite a bit. The car did go to that wharf—and that wharf is on the sea side of a Key. Boats could be rowed up to it. At high tide, one of the commercial fishermen's boats might get in. A light down there at night would be visible for several miles. But it does seem a devilishly un-likely and inconvenient place to bring anybody ashore. And if it was at all rough, it wouldn't be possible."

"Which may be the reason they use it. So unlikely."

"Quite." He drove frowningly. "What I must do, is reconnoiter."

"Reconnoiter? 'Way down here?"

"My vacation," he reminded her. "And it need be only on calm nights—as you point out. I'll watch."

"Shouldn't you go to the police?"

"They would laugh at me. We need definite information."

She shook her head. "You can't watch, Martin. Don't you realize the insects would eat you alive? Especially on the kind of nights when they could land there. Still nights. That's probably one more reason they use such a spot."

"Insects!" he said. "Mosquitoes and sand flies! One would hardly be rendered *hors de combat* by a few pests."

Ten:

IT DOES not require a profound philosophy to expose the ironies of life. And one of the ironies is this: the good deed of a good man may be observed by thousands and will be forgotten in a day, but any appearance of scandalous behavior in a decent citizen will get itself bruited about indefinitely. The good repute of Professor Burke was caught in this process, by an almost expectable chance. On the evening of his visit with Double-O Sanders, two undergraduates had been dancing in the patio of the Bombay Royale Hotel. As they came through the lobby to summon their car and start home, they saw two persons emerge from an elevator.

The girl undergraduate said, "Why—there's Professor Burke—and a babe! Who would have imagined such a thing?" Naturally, they hung back a little and thus observed the good-night kiss tendered to the professor by the young lady.

By evening of the day following, the story had progressed through a considerable portion of the student body.

Because of it, Miss Marigold Macey was listless the next morning at breakfast. Her mother noticed it as she quietly engineered the juice squeezer, the toaster, the percolator and the waffle griddle. Her brother noticed it vaguely as he studied the brief of a law case. And her father finally became aware of it as he perused the paper. It annoyed him.

"What in hell," he enquired, "is the matter with you?"

"Matter?" Marigold temporized.

"Nibbling at your waffle! Rolling toast crumbs!"

"Jizzling," her brother added, without looking up.

"Well," Marigold said, "I'm in love."

Both men now looked at her. Both said, "Again!"

"This time," the girl said morosely, "it's different."

"It's different every time," her mother murmured.

The judge glanced sharply at his wife—was caught doing it—and winked. His wife winked back.

"How different?" asked her brother, skeptically.

"He's older, Steve. I feel maternalish about him—and scary. And then . . ." she rolled crumbs.

"Then what?" her father asked.

Marigold spoke petulantly. "Don't cross-question me! Ye gods! When your father's a judge and your brother's a lawyer, a girl lives practically in the witness box!"

"You brought the matter up," Steve said.

"I did not!"

"Rolling crumbs and jizzling. Perjorative behavior."

"He goes around with Other Women," Marigold said slowly. "He was seen a few nights ago—necking one."

Judge Macey folded the paper neatly. "Marigold," he said, "did you ever hear of *quid pro quo?* I mean to say—what in the devil were you doing with that Stratton boy on the porch the other night? And the long list of his predecessors? Studying the nocturnal habits of the glowworm?"

Her mother saved her from answering. "Who is he?"

"Martin Burke."

The two men looked blankly at each other. Mrs. Macey explained. "He's one of her professors. Now, Simon! Contain yourself! I met him last year at a drainage meeting." She saw she had to explain that, too. "Everglades-draining problems. He's quite young—for a full professor. He's extremely attractive, too—although he doesn't seem to realize it. His manners are simply dazzling. And he comes from New England."

The judge said, "Really?" He looked at his daughter with interest.

"Bring him around," said Stephen. "Both ways."

Her father nodded. "This is the first time I

ever heard you worrying about what you somewhat hypocritically call 'other women.' It *must* be serious, by gad!"

Mrs. Macey smiled at a waffle. "With Professor Burke, I would imagine that pretty much everything is serious."

"It is not!" Marigold spoke with heat. "Do you call publicly necking a Miami Beach blonde, serious? And that's just one thing! Professor Burke only acts stuffy and superpolite. Actually—he's an authority on crime. He's been right in the midst of gang wars. He knows personally half the big shots in the underworld. He's two distinct personalities—and it's terribly fascinating."

"Nonsense," said her father. "A professor?"

"Drag him over here," Steve repeated.

"I've tried," she said.

Her brother snorted. "Lookie, cookie. If you try—he'll come. I don't know what it is. The big brown eyes, the well-made if slightly undersized chassis, or that wobble in your vocal cords. But they work, if you work them. Now, be a good kid and drag your prof over here."

She looked mournfully out of the French windows and down the arched patio, over the sun-polished Macey lawn to the garden hedge. "I'll try again," she said miserably.

Just exactly how he found himself walking home that afternoon with Marigold Macey, the professor could not be sure. He was preparing his work for the next term—a morass of pressing details. The strong easterly which had risen on Sunday evening might die down soon; if so, he would have to be absent from Coral Gables for a time. He was trying to get ready when Marigold appeared in his office.

She asked some trivial question about the work in the following term. She sat on his desk, patted his arm, batted her eyes, switched herself about, and urged him to accompany her home for tea. She did not call him, "honeychile"; a girl has to draw the line somewhere.

Her home was several blocks away, in the opposite direction from Bedelia's—and he found himself walking with the girl at his side. She seemed very happy. And he was not displeased. He recalled the unmistakable leer he had given her in the College Inn Tearoom, the notion that had prompted the grimace, and his subsequent conclusion that it had doubtless forever alienated Miss Macey. It seemed not to have done so. On the contrary.

As they walked, she talked of this and that. "You detest Miss Orme, don't you?" she said.

"There's something about her. The snood. Always reminds me of a beaver's tail."

Marigold chuckled. "Your star student—*but . . . !*"

"Intellectually overenergetic, if such a thing is possible." He smiled. "Going to be a social worker, she says. I have no doubt of it. I can imagine her thrusting principle and theory on the underprivileged—with all the whelming purposefulness of a bulldozer. I shouldn't make such a statement about a student. But Miss Orme . . . !"

"Not liking her, shows good taste in women."

"Really?" He had never viewed it from that angle.

"Of course! Don't be naïve!"

They reached her residence. "We'll go in the side and around to the garden," she said. "Tea won't be ready for a while—not till Dad's home."

The garden was hedge-enclosed and contained, besides a round pool where fishes swam and water lilies floated, some aluminum furniture and a barbecue fireplace. Marigold chose a languorous double chair and patted the place at her side. He sat. The sun was very low and the air was suffused with orange light.

She took his hand. "Nice of you to come over."

"I'm very glad I did it."

"I thought you sort of—disliked me."

"Nothing could be farther from the truth."

These, and some further platitudinous remarks, along with the warm feel of the girl's hand in his own, led to a recrudescence of a recent sentiment. It became so acute that he let go of her hand and rose with the thought of sauntering over to the pool. Marigold, however, interposed herself between him and the pool. *Why not?* his brain suggested. She was looking up at him with an extravagant brilliance in her eyes—which at least suggested she might consent to the experiment. He stepped forward, put his arms around her, and kissed her firmly, unprofessorially.

"Great gad, man!" the judge bellowed, coming through the hedge.

Professor Burke's mind rocketed back to what constituted reality for him. He loosened his hold of the girl. He thought of his situation in the terms in which he had been reared to think. The man with the grey temples, flushed face and irate voice was plainly her father. At that moment the professor felt passionately enamored of Miss Macey. So he said, rather croakingly, "My intentions are perfectly—"

"To hell with your intentions! You're trampling my pineapple!"

Professor Burke jumped.

Marigold, who was both pleased and astonished by the past twenty or thirty seconds of her existence, burst into laughter. "Father," she said, when she could, "is trying to sprout a pineapple." She pointed to its top—in a small, mulched bed. "Daddy, this is Martin Burke."

The judge said, "Delighted," fell to his knees, and began replacing the tilted plant. "Tea is ready," he continued. "The next time you decide to kiss anybody, Marigold, for heaven's sake keep out of the flower beds. I told your mother it would root—and by gad, it's rooting!"

A short week ago, Professor Burke would have regarded even the idea of amorously kissing a young lady as something to be pushed into the nebulous future. A short week ago, he would have regarded being caught doing just that, by the girl's father, as a shocking catastrophe. He was, however, changing.

"I got lipstick on you," Marigold said. "Hold still."

Even this did not utterly dishevel him. He intended to kiss her again, at the earliest opportunity. He had tried to say that his intentions were honorable—idiotic phrase!—and he now saw that they were merely to kiss her.

Judge Macey satisfied himself that the pineapple was not ruined. He rose—and shook hands. "Don't be embarrassed," he said. "My daughter's impulses are familiar to the whole family. She's really quite a nice girl—though headstrong. Come in and meet my wife and my son, Steve."

This, in the professor's opinion, was both the civil and the mature way of looking at the matter.

"I hear," the judge went on, "that you're a New Englander. So are we. Expatriates." No topic could have been more fortunate.

Throughout the tea which followed, they indulged in a kind of nostalgia—a fest of place names, of recipes, and of worrying over the spread of the Dutch elm disease on New England's commons. They found mutual friends—and, as was inevitable, Esperance Perthnot, who came to America just after the *Mayflower* and who was a remote ancestor of the Maceys as well as of the Burkes. Naturally, they invited the professor to stay for dinner; being a New Englander, he refused politely. Naturally, both he and his hosts realized that he would accept a later invitation.

When the professor had gone, stepping lightly into the bland dark, the judge said, "Marigold, I really believe you're growing up. That's a very intelligent young man."

She regarded her father demurely. "He can neck like hell, too!" It was a boast rather than a fact.

The judge was a New Englander, but aware of modern trends. Hence he took no umbrage. He looked his daughter steadily in the eye. "Of course he can neck like hell. Comes from good stock!"

"What were you and he talking about, when you spent so long showing him your den?"

The judge smiled. "He was asking my advice. Talking about what you called the—other side of his personality."

"Was he? What'd he say?"

"Just put a hypothetical question. Asked me what I would do if I had inside facts which led me to suspect that a certain group of men were engaged in a particularly nefarious and antisocial activity. Would I report my suspicions to the authorities? Or would I continue my observations until I confirmed them beyond doubt?"

"And what did you advise?"

The judge picked up the evening paper and walked to his easy chair. "It was a pretty nebulous question. I told him that I thought the 'authorities' would tend to regard the suspicions of a person like himself with a good deal of doubt—unless he had some very convincing evidence. After all, a professor running around to the police station talking about 'antisocial activities' . . . ! These Miami cops probably wouldn't know what he meant."

"Isn't he exciting!"

"I'm reading," her father answered rather plaintively. "Exciting? Burke? Sound as a rock! Nothing exciting about the man. Good chap!"

Eleven:

PROFESSOR BURKE sat down in the sea. It was nearly midnight. It was Christmas Eve. It was no time for a man to be wading—and now sitting—in the pitch-black ocean off the Florida Keys. The water was lukewarm over the flats, and there was no wind. The stars were glowing balefully. Near at hand loomed the underbrush on shore. Faraway, in the opposite direction, a lighthouse swept its pale, impalpable arms round and round forever, encircling nothing, revealing only the endless flicker of salt sea. Insane, he thought. He should be up at Bedelia's, opening their reciprocal gifts beneath her small, electric-lighted tree.

But the easterly had dropped that morning. The wharf would be usable. The fact was scant indication it would be used; it was, however, the only indication he had to go on. Christmas Eve might suit them.

Behind him, up the coast of Little Tango Key, his coupé stood on one of the roads they had explored. He had parked it there with the coming of darkness. He had eaten his sandwiches and cake and drunk coffee from his thermos in solitude. Every half hour he had walked down to the waterfront and looked. It was well past eleven when the lame man—presumably—had set a gasoline lantern on the little dock.

No one, as Bedelia had pointed out, could stand the torment of exposure in the underbrush or on the near-by water. The professor had worked out a protective device, based upon the bee-hat. He donned it—a helmet of fine screen which sat on his shoulders. It was painted a dull black. Fixed to it were numbers of wires covered with green paper, which Bedelia used for securing vines. Twisted in these wires were many small branches which the professor had picked before dark. He put on gloves.

In this regalia he was able to wade down the coast line. When he was satisfied that his wading sounds might soon be distinguished from the occasional splash of a fish, he moved out to sea. The bottom—now sandy, now oozy—slippery and then weedy—forced him to go very slowly. He found, finally, a spot with sandy bottom some fifty yards or so beyond the yellow-green, faintly hissing, gasoline lantern. He eased himself down.

There, his plans completed themselves. From anything but direct inspection, he was safe: above water, he looked like any clump of mangrove branches which floats in the currents around the Keys.

The lame man had left the dock. The night was quiet. He thought of sting rays and barracudas and morays. He reminded himself not to budge if some creature bumped against him. And not to cry out under any circumstances.

He forced his thoughts along rational channels: sting rays and morays did not attack unless disturbed—and barracuda struck seldom, under any conditions. It was much too shallow for large sharks.

He conquered his nerves and then thought about the Coral Gables Choir, which would still be caroling wherever a candle showed in a window. No snow—nothing here to suggest Christmas. No loose tire-chains clanking against fenders in the crystalline dark. No icicles hanging like glass stalactites around the eaves. Just people standing around amongst rosebushes, jasmine, hibiscus—to sing "Silent Night" and "Little Town of Bethlehem."

Small waves lapped around his portable greenery. Insects hummed indignantly outside his screen. He switched his thoughts to Marigold. Connie Maxson intruded. So he turned back to the matter of carols. Mentally, he hummed, "The First Nowell." He heard a washing, gurgling sound, out toward the open sea. Cautiously, he turned around.

For a long time, he saw nothing. Sea—stars— the remote lighthouse. Then he heard a car on the land. Its motor whined a little. He knew its wheels were sluicing in the soft, white marl. Feet sounded on the dock. He glanced back. Men were there now—two of them. The light had been dimmed.

He turned his attention toward the sluicing sound.

And suddenly it took form—a dark, huge shape, and a white combing at the water level. He heard the muffled voices of men, grunting. The thing came steadily nearer. He began to fear it would run him down. As he considered a retreat from the path of the great, black blob, he made it out. It had wings.

It passed him, slowly, splashingly, at a distance of a few rods. When it came between himself and the gasoline light, he could see it perfectly. A two-motored seaplane. Or amphibian. It bobbed and eddied as it was pushed toward the flimsy wharf by two men in the water. The propellers, he saw, were many bladed—and the blades were wide. They looked like the vanes of a windmill.

Somewhere he had read about just such propellers. They were said to be very quiet. Certainly, although the plane must have landed within a half mile of where he was concealed, he had not heard it. And naturally enough, it had showed no light. Instrument landing? Perhaps. Perhaps an accurate knowledge of the area—and a glint from the lighthouse, enough to show the pilot the sea surface. A plane with quiet propellers and, doubtless, engine-mufflers.

A windless night for a gentle landing—and this method of hand-taxing across the shoals. The coastal authorities, he reflected, would not think of the possibility of pushing a plane, by wading, across a mile of flats. It was, all in all, exceedingly ingenious.

The plane was swung around at the pier. A door opened.

"Howdy, Chuck."

"Hi, Solo. Six customers."

"Well—get 'em out. These bugs . . . !"

The professor watched the six passengers of the plane step out. They required help. He could soon see why: their hands were linked together behind their backs and they were bent forward, as if pulling against their hands.

Handcuffs, evidently, Then the professor could make out not only the glitter of the steel, but the sash weights which were wired onto the handcuffs. The cargo was disposable. Dropped overboard—from aloft, or in the deeper water—these passengers would vanish. No incriminating evidence.

They were rubbing their arms and hands, now. One of them sobbed, suddenly. "Shut up, sister!"

Another "passenger" asked something in a low tone.

"Naw, you damned hun! Not here. You got a long ride in a trunk compartment. Then you'll be in good old U.S.A. to celebrate Christmas. Only—you probably won't feel like it. Come on, guys. I'm being eaten alive!"

It was then that something struck the professor. Forcibly. It might have been a turtle. A ray. A bonefish hurrying in the night. It might have been any of a hundred creatures. He did not cry out.

But he lost his balance. He made a swimming motion with his hands to regain it. And the motion set up a sharp splash.

The men on the dock fell silent. A strong beam from a flashlight shot over the water and began sweeping in circles. The beam found the miniature greenery and held on it.

"Weeds," a voice said. "What's the matter? Spooky?"

"Fish," said another voice.

"Lemme look." The professor recognized it as the old man's. The light once more blinded him.

"People been pokin' around here lately," the old man said. "Maybe it is weeds. Looks kind of funny. Floats high. I'll send a bullet into it."

"Cut it out, you fool! Chuck! Johnny! Walk back in and take a squint at that bunch of weeds."

They came close. One carried a boat hook. The professor heard the other murmur, "Something in it, anyhow! Look in the water—underneath!"

"Shall I take a slam at it?"

With an emotion like cosmic self-censure rather than fear, the professor rose to his feet. "Never mind, gentlemen. I surrender."

The spectacle of the greenery lifting itself from the sea startled the two men. The professor thought of running. But he knew he could not run fast in water that deep. The light would be at his back. And the range would be easy. He started wading toward the little wharf.

When he got there, the six airplane passengers

92

were gone. The old man and a husky-looking, well-dressed fellow with sleek, black hair were alone on the dock. Each covered him with a gun. The younger man was slapping at his face with his free hand. "Take that thing off!"

The professor removed it. Light struck his eyes.

"That," said the old man, "is the same jerk came poking around here a few days back."

The professor's clothes dribbled. The two men from the plane, also dripping, came up beside him. The round, white stare of the flashlight was very close. "Who are you?" The voice was the younger one—cold, furious, afraid.

"Martin L. Burke—University of Miami. An amateur—interested in gang methods. I—"

Professor Burke heard a sound. The light danced. A hot feeling came in his cheek. His ear rang. He realized he had been hit—hit hard.

"Who? A Fed? Treasury? Customs? Talk fast!"

Professor Burke was panting, now. "I told you—"

They hit him again.

"Look in his pockets!"

"He wouldn't be carrying anything, Solo."

"Look anyhow."

They looked. The professor got his breath and his grip on himself.

"Put cuffs on him, Chuck. And drop him over—about halfway back. Whoever the hell he is!"

Twelve:

THE HANDCUFFS held his arms together behind his back. The weights—twenty-five or thirty pounds of them—pulled achingly. He was left standing on the wharf while Chuck and the other pilot— Johnny, the professor thought—went up on the bank and talked with Solo for a minute. Then he was pushed up the board and into the cabin of the plane. He heard the car leave.

They used the flashlight briefly, in order to tie him into a seat. Then they went out the door and onto the nose of the plane. He heard their splashes. Slowly, the plane turned.

He had a glimpse through the door of the lame old man, carrying the gasoline lantern away. Then it was dark. The door shut quietly.

For a long while, the plane moved in slow surges out across the flats. Then it rocked as the two men clambered back on board. They threw a light on him and checked the knots they had made.

One of them then thrust his head through the hatch and turned in a complete circle, slowly. "Coast's clear."

Forward in the plane, a very faint light now glowed. The man put down a heavy pair of binoculars. Presently, there was a tick and a cough and one engine started. It was astoundingly quiet. The professor did not hear the other motor fire and take hold. He simply felt the plane start along the smooth sea, gather speed, and, at last lift itself.

They flew for what the professor had estimated as twenty minutes and then one of them turned on a meagre light in the cabin. He stripped off his wet clothes, toweled himself, and brought dry garments from some point in the rear of the ship. He put them on.

"Okay, Chuck!"

The other pilot now changed his clothes.

When he was dressed, he sat down across from the professor. It was so dim that only his square profile, the gleam of his eyes, and his crewcut hair could be discerned.

His voice was flat. "All right. Who are you?"

"I told you. A college professor interested in criminology. I've made a hobby of gangs. I have nothing whatever to do with the police, the F.B.I., or any other such agency."

The man called Chuck sat quietly for a moment and then moved a little. Something glittered in his hand. "I know a guy," he said, "who has a jack-knife, like this one. When he wants people to talk to him—he uses it. Just the tip. That's the name of the guy: The Tip. He just uses the tip—under fingernails, to start with. After the tip of his knife has loosened up ten fingernails, a person has ten

95

toenails. Doesn't kill a person. Just seems to make them talk. If nails don't work, a person has eyeballs . . ."

"I told you the truth."

"Maybe you did. It's just that I don't believe it. Talk some more." He leaned over and seized one of the professor's hands. The professor felt the knife point slide under his nails and into the quick. For a moment, it was a mere shock. Then the pain came.

"I've been studying the Maroon Gang a long time," he said, when he felt he could talk evenly again. "I'll tell you some of the things I know about it. I'm a scientist—not a cop. I'll tell you things that the cops don't know. When I do, you'll see that I am what I say."

Chuck said, "So shoot."

Professor Burke had been thinking feverishly. He had dismissed from his mind the near certainty that the plane would be throttled down, the door would be opened, and he would be pitched out, to fall an unimportant number of thousand of feet, to land with a violence that would surely knock him senseless and probably kill him, and thereafter to be pulled down by the weights through two or three more thousand feet of Gulf Stream. No trace. No body to be recovered.

But Bedelia would know what to do.

It followed, therefore, that they would need to discover who he was and what his connections were—how much of his information was already known to others. They would be stupid to pitch him over without questioning. The questioning methods would be drastic. What, then, to tell them? What would be most effective? He had settled on the truth—with limitations.

He began, now, to talk to Chuck about the Maroon Gang. He had a grim abundance of information on the theme, supplied by Double-O. He had selected certain high spots. As he talked, his manner became discursive. Soon, he was lecturing. His right index finger throbbed, but no more fingers were adding to the pain—yet.

For perhaps a half hour, Chuck merely listened. But he listened with gathering awe. No man lacks interest in the hidden lore of his own occupation or in the low-down on his betters. The professor was capitalizingon that fact. Finally, Chuck began to comment.

"So they bought the Police Commissioner?"

"And six months later sank him in cement, in a river."

Chuck whistled at another point. "They shot Lorrie?"

"—but he didn't die. He's living in Mexico."

"The girl did that?" he asked, again.

The professor nodded. "Yes. Sarah Brown—nobody ever knew her real name—did precisely that."

It was the other pilot who finally stopped the eerie talk. He looked back and called, "Hey! We're halfway over! And then some!"

Chuck said a doubtful, "Yeah." He peered at the professor. "How come you never gave that to the coppers?"

"I told you I'm a scientist—not a stool pigeon."

"Be damned!" The man chuckled. "Some of the things you told me—it is going to be mighty handy for me to know. I can use 'em if I ever need to."

"I was sure you could," the professor said. "I told you because I don't want to get dumped in the sea."

That surprised the man with the crew haircut. "Yeah? I thought you were just—keeping clear of the tip of the knife. Mister, you get dumped. That's all there is to that!"

The professor, like every man, had speculated many times on what he would think, feel, do, when his hour came. Here it was. And he found himself analytical. He was relieved that his death—although dramatic—would not be overly painful or long-drawn. One finger would hurt as he somersaulted down the thousands of feet. He wondered how long Bedelia would wait for him before going into action. He could think of nothing else to help himself. His back and arms were beginning to ache so much that his finger—given time—would have been the lesser pain. He knew now—very completely—why the six smuggled aliens had stretched and rubbed themselves and hardly seemed to notice the mosquitoes, when they had come ashore.

Now the man named Johnny said, "Hey, Chuck! Get set!"

The motors were cut down. The professor could feel the air push against the plane like a brake. Chuck went to the door. Something squeaked. He was prying it open against the streaming air, with a crowbar. Cold wind rushed in. The professor shivered in his sodden clothes. *Somebody*, he thought, *everybody, in fact, should be made to understand the ferocity of the criminal.*

His own efforts—his lectures, his book—had been pitiably inadequate. In the presence of the fact, all theory was inane. He deserved in a sense, the pitch into blackness which was coming. Chuck began to untie the knots that held him in the seat.

Thirteen:

As THE SECONDS trickled, Professor Burke found in himself a sudden, tremendous anger. They might have thrown many people out of their plane and down to the sea when they had a signal that landing was inadvisable. And those people might have died submissively. They had come a long way through risks and hardships; the last leg of their illicit journeys might have brought death; and they might have half-expected it. But Professor Burke knew he was not going to jump willingly through the door where the wind howled. They had guns. But he might take a lot of killing. It was murky in the plane. He would move as fast as he could.

"Okay," Chuck said.

The professor stood, "Could I have—a last cigarette?"

"Hell, no. Get up."

He gathered his feet under him.

And Jonny turned from the controls. "Hey!" He took off earphones. "Hold everything."

"What's the matter?" Chuck asked sharply.

"Call coming in!"

"Put on on the speaker."

Static crackled, Chuck kept his eyes on the professor and listened.

"Miami Marine Operator," a metallic, female voice said harshly. "Calling the yacht *Mary Fifth.*"

There was a wait. Then a man's voice, fainter. "Yacht *Mary Fifth.* Go ahead please!"

"Here's your party!" the Operator said.

Professor Burke realized that the plane was equipped with a radio which enabled it to pick up ship-to-shore phone conversations. Any boat with ship-to-shore apparatus could listen to all others; whoever telephoned from land to a fishing boat at sea, for example, made a call public to all other fishing boats. And public also to this plane.

"How's fishing, Hank? This is Paul."

The Professor's skin prickled. It was *French Paul.*

The faint voice answered heartily, "Pretty Good! We're trolling off Virginia Key, now. Doing okay. Some tarpon around here."

"You got one?"

There was a pause. "What say? Over!"

"I said—you got one?"

"Sure."

"Got him in the live well?"

"Yeah. We got one in the live well. Over."

"See if you can bring him back, will you? To put in the pond at my place. Over."

"Okay. We'll try it."

"Coming in after an hour or so?"

"Yeah. Hour or so."

101

"Well—we'll have something to eat up here for you. Stop by our dock. And bring us a tarpon if he'll stay alive in the well."

"Okay. Will do."

"Well—good fishing!"

"Roger! *Mary Fifth*. Signing off."

Chuck talked inaudibly with Johnny for a minute. Then he strode past the professor and removed the block with which he had jammed open the door. He came back.

"Want those weights off, professor?"

"I—don't get it."

Chuck took a key from his pocket. A lock clicked. The professor's arms were free. He was able—barely—to move them into his lap. He began chafing them.

"Pretty cute?" Chuck asked, then.

"I'm not quite sure I understand—"

Chuck laughed. "You know so damn much! You should be wise to this! On the nights we fly, maybe the *Mary Fifth*—that's a Miami boat—goes out fishing. Or maybe just out for a moonlight trip with some guys and gals. She keeps tuned to the Marine Operator. And we keep tuned, too. If anybody wants to send us a message—you know who—they just raise the *Mary Fifth* on the ship-to-shore phone. Then they do a little double-talk about fishing or late supper or a charter of the next day or something. What they talk about, means different things to us. See?"

"Yes."

"Like—suppose there were Feds nosing around Little Tango Key . . ."

"I get it."

Chuck was pleased with the system. "Tonight they want a live tarpon brought in—just in case we have a live tarpon on board. That Ely sure caught on fast to what he was supposed to say. Anyhow, the boss wants a live tarpon in his pond. And you're it."

The man in wet clothes with stiff arms smiled barrenly. "I see how it works, now."

Chuck laughed again. "They could listen for secret radios till doomsday. We communicate right over the regular public telephone system!"

"Very ingenious. And very timely."

"What? Brother! Was it! Old Paul's tarpon darn near fell overboard!" He slapped the professor's shoulder.

The plane flew. By and by Chuck took the controls and Johnny stood—or sat—watch on the professor. Johnny had light hair and he was thin. A silent silhouette. The professor did not feel like talking anyway. He continued to rub his wrists and arms.

He was conscious of the descent. The landing was expert. This time, a rope was thrown to the plane and a rowboat toiled in the darkness until the bottom grated. Chuck opened the door. *"Señores,"* he called softly. *"Com esta?"*

"Muy buen."

The professor was taken to the door, between

103

the two pilots. He was turned around; he felt with his foot for a step. Then he was on shore.

It was as dark in Cuba as it had been in the Keys. Cuba, he felt certain. Double-O had mentioned Cuba. The men in the boat spoke Spanish. The the flying time was probably right for it—long, perhaps. There were men about, talking softly in the dark. Two of them gripped his arms.

"See you, Professor!" Chuck called softly.

They went for a distance on a dirt road. Then they were among houses with an occasional light. One of the men who held him said in his ear, "You are drunk, if anybody appear. You stagger. We will laugh—your *amigos*—taking you home."

They walked from the dark street into a less dark one. Down a side street, he heard laughter, and a rumba band. Over a radio, in a building that seemed dead of its age, he also heard a snatch of Christmas music.

It was not a large town. Some little Cuban seaport. They took him around another corner and through a narrow arch. It led to the inner court of a big building. Tall trees grew there. A fountain dribbled. The place smelled of mold and human generations. A door was opened and he was hurried up a turning flight of stone steps. Another door, unlocked with an imminse, old-fashioned key.

He was pushed through this door and it closed.

He expected to find himself in a prison—orobably a windowless chamber, possibly without a light, and certainly alone.

There were four people in the room, sitting around a kerosene lamp on a a table. One was a woman—brunette, young, very pretty. One was an extremely old man, with a white beard. the other two were in their thirties or forties. The windows were high and boarded up. Open luggage lay about.

The woman said, *"Bien venu, ami—et joyeux noel!"*

The professor thought, *the next load.*

"You are wet." The old man said it calmly. "Franz. We could lend him dry clothing."

"Ja wohl."

The third man stared blankly at the professor. "Who are you?" he finally said.

The woman laughed. "The old one"—her English was heavily accented—"is called Herr Wasser. So Franz is also Wasser. This other has no name. I am Lorraine Dumond." Franz was rummaging in a suitcase. "I will turn my back," the girl continued.

The professor demurred. "Really—my clothes will dry. It is a warm evening. My name is Burke, incidentally."

The man called Franz Wasser smiled a little. "Go ahead. We are to leave the baggage in any case. These are good garments. English. Use the small bath."

Reluctantly, embarrassedly, the professor changed.

The old man watched for his return. "The finger bleeds," he said.

They all looked at his finger. "A splinter," he said. "I had to climb—then to swim."

"I have some . . ." the girl did not know the name. But she went to her own suitcase and brought a bottle of peroxide with a French label.

"Iodine," said the third man, "is better."

He offered iodine.

Professor Burke nodded. The bottle produced by the third man had no label. The man put cotton on a match stick. He dipped it and probed the wound with needless force. The professor turned grey, but his finger did not shake.

The man said, "That will be sufficient." He had quite dark skin, but light hair.

The man with the beard began to read a book printed in German. His son Franz walked over to a rickety cot and lay down, closing his eyes. The man who had no name sat at the table again and became immersed in his thoughts. They had accepted the professor, taken him for granted. He chose a chair in the corner. There were several in the room.

Presently the girl walked over to him. "Be cheerful," she said. "Six went this very evening."

"Splendid!"

"You have been in—America?"

He looked at her steadily. "I lived there for some years. It seems a long time ago."

"*Moi—jamais*. I am excited."

"It is an extraordinary country—"

"It is," said the nameless man, "a hell!"

The old man spoke, "Shall we sleep, friends?"

They took places—a chair—another rag-covered cot—and the nameless man on the floor. The bearded man blew out the kerosene light.

Fourteen:

PROFESSOR BURKE thought about them for a while. Who were they? Spies? Perhaps. People escaping the shambles of their world. *Nazis who had got away the loot.* That might fit Herr Wasser and his thin son. Who was the nameless man? The bleak, grey eyes, the overzealous application of iodine, the chilly confidence in himself. He could be anybody.

In the dark, the professor woke and wondered where he was. He remembered slowly, and slept again. The next time he woke, he remembered instantly. There were footsteps outside the door.

It was a man with a gun—a Cuban—and a fat woman with a heavy tray. She said, *"Buenos dies, señores y señora!"* She put down the tray. Fried fish and boiled rice, a long loaf of bread, butter, and coffee.

The professor took his turn in what a better class of hostelry would have called the "adjoining bath." It had no windows. The plumbing was a European import of the nineteenth century. The only light was a candle, which each one lit and each blew out. He washed his face. His finger was sore, but not throbbing.

108

After breakfast, as if they had done it many times, the nameless man walked under the windows and lifted Franz until he could put his ear against the crack in the boards. It was a feat of considerable strength.

Franz listened. "I hear nothing," he said.

The girl explained to the professor needlessly. "We fly—as you must know. But only in the still weather."

"Once," said the old man, "so we were told, there were fifty people here. The wind blew many weeks without stopping. They showed us how to listen."

The nameless man sat silently all morning with his nameless thoughts. Herr Wasser and his son played chess, under the lamp. The girl began a low conversation. "When the Nazis came to my town," she said, "I married an officer. I collaborated, they say, though I did nothing but marry the enemy. When France was liberated, I had become a Displaced Person in Germany. My husband had left some money in the Argentine. It took two years for me to get there. But coming to America openly is hopeless. So . . ." she shrugged. "My jewels paid this passage."

During the morning, the Wassers told a somewhat similar story to him, told it mechanically, in detail so that he realized it was not the truth. They claimed to have been anti-Hitler Germans.

The nameless man said nothing.

About noon, the door opened. Two Cubans

beckoned. The professor was escorted to a room down the dark, tiled hallway. It was a smaller room, well furnished and electrically lighted. More men sat in it—men he had never seen. Americans. One of these was bald and bug-eyed. He did the talking.

"My name is Wilser. Sit down, Professor."

He looked pasty, the professor thought. Like a big-eyed larva.

"Paul," said Wilser, "was unable to cover over this morning. I have talked with Chuck and Johnny." He hesitated. "Your knowledge of our—organization—surprised me. How did you come by it?"

Professor Burke smiled a little. If he had thought that his removal from the room of the aliens was a hopeful sign, he did not think so now. Not after looking at Wilser. "The way I found out all I know. Watching. You hardly need a diagram of my methods. Your men uncovered them."

"How did you know about the Foot's dock?"

"Haven't you figured that out?"

"We know you and that horse-faced landlady of yours were down there looking for ferns. Now. Tell us how you got onto it. We want to keep it from happening again."

The professor smiled once more, slightly. "In that case, Mr. Wilser, before you drive your cars north from the Keys you should wash the white marl off their wheels. And you better cut back the ferns along the road to the dock. They are a spe-

cial kind of fern—a sort of sport of a Glades ge-
nus—which is peculiar only to a few, small Keys."

"Where'd you see a car—with marl and these
ferns?"

"You might ask French Paul."

Wilser thought that over. "Oh." His eyes lighted
unpleasantly—as if there were little hot places in
them. "Naturally," he then said, "we went right
after that landlady of yours."

Professor Burke's heart turned to stone.

"Is there anybody else?" Wilser asked.

"Nobody."

"We want to be quite sure of that, Professor.
Quite sure. We intend to be—before . . . !
There's another matter. Chuck has told me some
details of your knowledge of the Maroon Gang.
Paul thought that under the existent circumstances
you might be willing to write it out for us. Make
everything less—painful—for you, in the end."

"I'll write it out."

"Every angle you know. There are several
that Paul would find very interesting, I think.
Singular information. Who gave it to you? Double-
O Sanders?"

"I told you, I've spent years in—research."

"It doesn't matter. You can work in the room
with our waiting clients. It's—secure. How long
will it take?"

The professor said, "A couple of days."

"Days!"

"I know a lot about the Maroon Gang."

Wilser thought that over. He turned to one of the men. "Okay. Give him the stuff to write with and a table of his own. Another lamp. Pick up his copy from time to time. I'll see you again, Professor."

He spent the afternoon writing.

The other people in the room did not question or interfere. They were accustomed to holding back questions and to avoiding interference. The members of the Maroon Gang would have many reasons for wanting to know all they could of their predecessors, associates and contacts. Blackmail was only one.

As he wrote, the professor paused frequently —apparently to recall details of his subject. Actually, he was thinking. They had Bedelia. They had no intention of letting him go alive. Bedelia might already be—gone.

Before dinner, Franz and the man without a name listened for the wind. It had not risen. This fact put three of the foreigners in a state of eagerness; the nameless man did not show any emotion. The professor went on writing into the evening. His ink-covered pages had been collected several times.

It might have been eight o'clock.

He needed three things. One of them could stay where it was; he could get it if he had the right opportunity.

He quit writing and went over the the nameless man. "Tovarich!" he said sharply.

The man looked up instantly. It was the only undeliberate move the professor had seen him make. Not proof of anything, except that the man knew Russian.

"Could I borrow your iodine again? My finger —I am afraid it may be getting infected."

The man did not speak at all. He rose, went over to his suitcase, and came back with the bottle.

"I will soak it," the professor said, "in a little iodine and water."

He took the bottle to the antediluvian bathroom. He poured about half of it in one of the two dirty glasses of the washbowl and hid the glass behind the battered bathtub. He diluted the iodine in the bottle with water, and—after delaying—returned it with thanks.

The man accepted it inexpressively.

The professor sat down beside the French girl.

She was nervous. They were all nervous. For, if their illicit conveyers found themselves watched, or if they became suspicious in any fashion, the aliens would not be smuggled into the United States. They would die. They knew it—or feared it.

The girl welcomed his talk. She asked questions about life in America. Was hailing a taxi the same as in France? Eating in a restaurant?

He explained the various restaurant check systems. He told her about cafeterias.

Her compact and lipstick were in the chair at her side. He made a half dozen furtive stabs at stealing the former before he got it. He put it in the pocket of the borrowed slacks he was still wearing. By and by he grimaced. "My finger. I will soak it again."

He transferred half of her powder to a folded sheet of writing paper which he had prepared. Then he came back. She hadn't missed the compact and she did not see him replace it. He went back to his work.

Time crawled. It was growing more and more difficult to keep his mind on the history of the Maroon Gang. He thought of Bedelia and the thought stiffened his will. Shortly after midnight, the door was opened. There were several men in the murky hall—among them, Chuck. They carried two lanterns.

"Everybody get set! Five minutes!"

Frantically, they rummaged for the last time through their treasures. The old man stuffed photographs into a pocket. The girl went into the adjoining room and the nameless man followed next. It was a better chance than the professor had hoped for; he slipped in the room

The man struck a match and walked toward the candle.

The professor bent down and slid his hand along the floor. He found the rusty wrench that he had decided was the best available weapon. He did not know how hard to hit.

The candle was lighting. The professor struck.

114

The man made no sound, but he shook from head to foot and kept standing.

He struck again. The man's scalp began to bleed. He sagged. The professor caught him.

He moved swiftly now. He shut the door. He picked up the hidden tumbler of diluted iodine and poured some of it over his face. He dried it with a filthy towel and peered into the mirror. His skin was dark, now—Indian dark. He washed his hands in the rest of the solution and wiped them. They were dark, also. He took the paper of powder from his pocket and sprinkled it in his hair. He rubbed his hair furiously and combed it with his fingers. It looked grey rather than hemp-color like that of the man on the floor.

He bent over the man. There was nothing in his trousers pockets. The professor stripped off his coat, donned it, and dragged the man to a dark corner. He was breathing; the professor took time to listen for that.

Now he strode to the candle and blew it out.

He opened the door a crack. They were talking—even laughing—laughing with a creepy, hysterical sound.

The outer door was unlocked once more.

"All right, you! Come ahead!"

The professor walked boldly into the room and across it. The girl had gone first—the old man and Franz were right behind her. He joined them.

"Where's the other one?" Franz asked. "Weren't you both . . . ?"

The professor gathered himself. This was the first of an unknowable number of crises. "He said —he was not to come with us." He had made his voice low like the voice of the unconscious man.

Chuck spoke. "The professor's staying," he agreed. He slammed the door and turned the big key.

They went down the turning staircase and through the patio with the huge trees. Into the street—walking together—with men ahead and men behind.

Light hair, dark skin, the same height, though the Russian—if he was one—was broader. Smelling of a woman's face powder and iodine. Unfortunate, but inevitable. He would see. They crossed streets, turned corners, passed the old buildings, the shops closed for the holidays, the radio behind the ancient walls. They left the small town for the soft road. A warm night—very warm for Christmas, even in Cuba. Still and starlit.

Trees closed above the road. A dull flashlight prodded the jungle, up ahead. Presently, it touched the open door of the plane. When the French-speaking girl realized what the weighted handcuffs meant, she screamed. Someone put a hand over her mouth. One by one, they went aboard, clanking a little.

The professor recognized Johnny's silhouette in the murky cabin. *Better than Chuck,* he thought.

He need not have worried. Johnny used his flashlight only to tie them to their seats. He sat

116

down in their rear. "Any fuss, and you are tossed out. Okay, Chuck!"

The quiet engines started. The plane taxied and lifted. All the long way, nothing was said.

The professor listened—listened for the crackle of static and the flat voice of the Miami Marine Operator. Listened for some amiable discussion with a fishing boat which might convey to the men in the plane that one of their passengers was an impostor. It did not come.

The plane descended. The professor expected the two men to jump overboard and begin pushing. But Chuck taxied the plane for some distance. Then there came a feeling of coasting and a gentle arrestation. Hands had gripped the wings. Johnny opened the door.

The next crisis was at hand.

They were herded ashore. The handcuffs were unlocked and the weights removed. The girl wept quietly.

It was, as far as the professor could make out, a lake, of some size, with a grassy shore and trees behind the grass. A small dock. Lanterns. The same man who had driven down to the Keys on the night before—husky, with patent-leather hair. Solo, they had called him.

They were walked along the dock, to the trees. A car stood there, a car different from the black sedan. In the lantern light he saw it was greenish. Big.

"The old bird and the girl can sit in back with Cliff," Solo said. "You two—in the truck."

The rear compartment lid yawned. Franz climbed in. The professor followed. Solo said, "Duck." They ducked—and the lid came down.

The road was atrocious. They banged into each other. The floor came up and struck them. They slid about. A better road came, finally. They lay still, panting. The tires whirred. The car was going fast.

Another eternity passed.

The car stopped, waited, and started. Traffic began to stir and horns to blow around them. They were getting into Miami.

Finally, the smooth pavement gave way to another rough ride—very short. Once more, the car stopped.

This time, the rear compartment was opened.

There was no light. Stars overhead—treetops —underbush. "All right, you guys. Get up!"

Franz and the professor painfully climbed over the bumper. The girl and the old man were gone.

Solo did not bother to use his flashlight.

"Listen. You both understand English."

"Very well," Franz said. The professor grunted.

"Oke. Now, get this. You're on a street that leads to a main highway. When we leave—start moving. Separate before you get to the highway. If the cops ever pick you up—you don't know anything about who got you here—or how. See?

Not that you know much. But one of you tell any-thing, and we've got an organization that can make you regret it, wherever you are." He turned, "Let's go, Cliff."

The big green car drove away. The delivery was completed. "Comfortable trip!" Franz murmured. "Shall we go?" He laughed a little. "I am a free American citizen! Living with my retired father, I knew you were one of the Soviet lice, the day you came in there."

"It is a poor time for that argument," the pro-fessor said. The highway appeared ahead of them. Occasional cars, busses, street lights. He was home again. And alive.

Fifteen:

FRANZ WENT out on the highway first. He had dusted off his clothing and made himself presentable. He walked to a painted lamp post and waited. The professor watched him board a bus.

He had recognized his surroundings: Brickell Avenue—about a mile from the business district.

He did not have bus fare. He had no plans. He began walking. Nobody seemed to be following. Nobody much seemed to be on the street. *Christmas Night,* he thought.

A police cruise car passed.

He had an impulse to yell at it.

Then what? The Station. Questioning. Delay. Doubts. More waiting for higher authority, perhaps. Christmas Night—and higher authority unwilling to leave festivities. He was without any proof of his story. They might even think he was crazy—iodine on his face—powder in his hair. And there was Bedelia.

He stepped into the gutter and thumbed. The cars swished past—on their way home from late evenings in the night clubs, from parties in homes, from pleasure and safety and an innocence of the

120

world. Then a car stopped. A dark face leaned out and a soft voice said, "Ride, friend?"

They were colored people on their way to Coconut Grove. "Drop you anywhere, mister," the driver offered.

The women in the back seat said nothing.

He picked the closest point on their route and walked from there. Coral Gables was mostly asleep. It was late for the Gables, even on that day. He left the sidewalks of West Cortez Circle at the distance of several houses and went through back yards. They might, by now, be expecting him.

There was a light in Bedelia's home.

He stood in the shadows of their neighbor's garage and looked—not daring to hope that Bedelia was there, fearing to investigate. His feelings overcame his judgment. He was about halfway through her leafy yard when a man stepped in front of him. A man with a gun. "What do you want, bud?"

"I—I live here." The professor hated himself.

"Yeah? You Burke?"

"I'm Burke."

"Come along." The man followed the professor to the porch. He knocked. After a while Bedelia called, "Yes? What is it?"

"Guy here says he's this Burke. I got him covered."

He heard the downstairs couch creak He heard her big, boney feet cantering in the hall. The porch

121

light switched on. "Martin! Thank heaven!" They embraced.

She addressed the man with the gun. "Thank you, Dusty. Keep a sharp eye out for anybody else."

"Okay, Miss Ogilvy." The night ate him.

She hurried the professor into the kitchen.

"What on earth have you done to yourself?"

"It's a long story," he said, grinning at her fondly. "Who's your guard?"

"That's a story, too."

He sat down at the familiar enamel-topped table. "They told me, in Cuba, that they'd caught you. Well—not exactly. That they'd gone after you."

She was staring. "*Cuba!*"

"I've been over the whole route," he answered. "Is the coffee hot?"

"It's been hot—pretty steadily, since early Christmas morning, Martin." Her spectacles misted up and she polished them on the hem of her kimono.

"I'm not sure we're safe—even with that guard."

"We've got three of them," she answered.

"Three! What are they? Private detectives?"

"My story will keep."

"And mine will take a long time. I need to know about the guards."

She looked at him—at his powdered hair, his face and hands, yellow-brown from the diluted iodine, and at his unfamiliar garments. She sighed.

122

"Just to reassure you, Martin. And I hope I did right." She poured coffee in her two largest cups. "I didn't expect you till some time in the morning. By ten o'clock, when no word came, I began to worry. You'd had time to drive back—after sunrise. It was possible, of course, that you were on to something that prevented your return or even making a phone call. But it was also possible that they'd caught you at it."

His eyes were grim—and the odd color of his face emphasized the fact. "They did."

"Oh, Martin . . . !"

"Take it easy, Bedelia. I'm right here, now."

"Well. I reasoned that if they had caught you, they might be after me. Correct, wasn't it? I closed up the house. But first I put hairs across several doors, with Scotch tape. My mother did it to jam closets. Then I went to the Duffys for Christmas dinner. I came back with them—the whole family—to show them our Tree. I felt nobody would bother two carloads of people and nobody did. But the hairs on the doors were broken, so I knew they had been here. When the Duffys left, I also went.

"I couldn't think what to do. I wanted to be at home—in case you arrived—and I was afraid to be there alone. I couldn't call the police—"

"You should have!"

Bedelia looked at him. "Then—why aren't you?"

"Go on."

123

"I felt I couldn't because you might return and it might be premature. Finally, in the late afternoon, I got hold of Mr. Sanders. I told him that you had gone looking into something and weren't back. I told him my house had been searched and I was worried about staying there. I asked if he could possibly send me a man or two to stand watch. He was delighted to help out."

"Good heavens!"

"He did ask me what you were doing—and I said I had no idea. I think he finally concluded that I was an overnervous woman. But he sent three dandy men. They arrived—at Laura's, where I was then—around five. I came over here with them and that's all. Now you talk!"

At the conclusion of a story that left Bedelia numb, he looked at the telephone. "I suppose I must call the police, or the F.B.I., or both of them —now. And yet I hate to. What I have found out will cause the arrest of a lot of underlings. French Paul and that detestable Wilser and a hundred more will probably get out of it. The whole, hideous thing should be untangled quietly for a while. And I'm absolutely exhausted. I don't know how I can even go to police headquarters—or any place—and answer hours of questions."

"I wouldn't, then. I'd go right upstairs and get a good night's sleep. Morning's sleep. Then you can go to the head of the F.B.I. Right now there wouldn't be anybody on duty but a clerk of some sort. A minor person. And the police—

from what Double-Q says—aren't to be relied on entirely. You might be giving information to one of them who would pass it straight to the Maroon people."

He thought about it. "I believe you're right, Bedelia."

"I'm sure of it! Anyone who tried to come in here after us tonight would get hurt!"

He lowered himself into his tub. He was bruised, scratched, strained—sore from head to foot. He scrubbed at his hands and face without much success. He nearly fell asleep.

The trousers of Franz Wasser and the jacket of the nameless man lay on a chair in his bedroom. He picked them up, sat tiredly on his bed, and examined them. No labels. The customers of the Maroon Gang were careful about labels. The jacket was rather thick. He squeezed it—and went to his bureau for scissors. He ripped the lining. Inside was a second, double lining of black cloth. Stitched in sections were ten one thousand dollar bills and many hundred dollar bills. The professor was becoming accustomed to such sums. He started to the stairway door to call Bedelia. He decided the fact would wait till they had slept. He tossed the jacket with the stitched-in money onto a chair. His bed creaked just once.

In a little-patronized, old-fashioned hotel in the coastal town of Vellehomez, in Cuba, the owner of the coat—the nameless man—came into a numb consciousness about an hour after a plane had quietly taken off.

The man's head hurt. He reached out and felt walls. One wall was cold and smooth. He remembered the antique tub. He remembered everything, then.

His coat was gone. That fact filled him with fury. The plane for America would be gone too. He got to his feet and found the door.

The kerosene lamps were still burning in the big room. No one was there. Abandoned luggage lay about.

He walked over to the larger table and took matches back to the bathroom. He lighted the candle. He looked at himself in the mirror. His hair was sticky. He started to wash. Then he noticed the diluted iodine spilled on the dirty, cracked sink—and the face powder on the floor.

He peered at his own face for a moment, and thought about the last one to arrive: Burke—the man who had spent most of the day scribbling something which their guards had taken away, every few hours. Burke—whoever he was—had dark hair and a light skin. Iodine and powder would reverse those characteristics. They were the same height and build.

The nameless man knew what had happened —although not why. The other, whom he had estimated to be something of a fool, had gone in his place. His rage increased.

Without the money, without the coat and its lining, his arrival in America would be a mistake. He would have to return, now, to Havana—and explain to Borston. Borston would be enraged. Moscow would be bitter.

To live his life—to put behind his career—and then to be slugged by a mild-looking capitalist imbecile!

He combed his hair without a grimace. He went into the big room and sat. He waited; he could wait.

The guards who came were unfamiliar. Two of them. Slight men and tipsy. It was Christmas Night, the nameless man reflected. *Bourgeois sentimentalists*.

He asked, in Spanish, for their chief.

"He has gone home to his wife—his children —long since, Professor."

"Well, I must leave. My plans are changed. I will not wait for the next trip."

"Leave, Professor?" They laughed.

He decided that it would be futile to try to explain the substitution to them. And he understood why Burke had impersonated him. They picked up the last few sheets that Burke had written. The nameless man wished he had read them.

He watched for an opportunity—and lunged.

He had overestimated his own condition and the drunkeness of the guards. One shouted and the other stepped aside. A knife flashed. The man without a name sank slowly to his knees and fell suddenly on his face.

"Idiot!" said one of the Latins.

"He would have killed me!"

"We must get word to Julio. He will be like a whip!"

At two o'clock in the morning, a phone rang in the Havana hotel room of Wilser. He answered and listened.

"If they had to," he finally said, "they had to. You know the procedure." He hung up and turned on the light. *More work to do.*

Long before daybreak, a handcart rumbled through the silent back streets of Vellehomez. It ceased rumbling when its wheels touched the dirt road. At the water front where, not very long before, the plane had taxied quietly into the harbor, a body was lifted from the cart into a skiff. Handcuffs with weights were fastened to the body. The skiff rowed slowly across the harbor. Its oarlocks did not squeak. The sea beyond was calm —and very deep. The body sent up a long chain of sound, the muttering of bubbles.

An amateur radio operator in the suburbs of Havana got in touch with a brother "ham" in America. They chatted cheerfully and familiarly of various matters, for a long time.

In the Bayfront residence of French Paul, two men played gin rummy. They had been playing, off and on, all night. They always did. A telephone buzzed. One of them answered and asked questions. Finally he switched the call to an upstairs bedroom.

French Paul woke, as Wilser had wakened less than an hour before. French Paul listened.

One of the men had come up from downstairs.

The fat Alsatian hung up and thought for a long time. Finally, he smiled. He threw back the covers of his bed.

"Our professor," he said, "has met with a mishap. He was a clever man. A little too—enterprising." He walked over to a desk, yawned, and sat down. "A friend," he said, "must send condolences—and a warning—to his landlady. The police in Vellehomez can announce the rest."

French Paul chuckled.

Sixteen:

BEDELIA HAD dressed, served, breakfast to Double-O's men, and was dusting when the mail truck drove up. Her guards did not interfere with the arrival of the special delivery letter. It contained one sheet, of single-spaced typewriting with neither salutation nor signature:

Professor Burke committed suicide last night near the town of Vallehomez, Cuba, after writing a confession of his jewel-smuggling. He was seen to leap from a skiff. His body was not found. Portions of a full confession—in his own hand—were recovered. So this letter may be regarded as an amicable warning. He had led you to believe he was hunting for certain persons—rather than acting as a member of a criminal organization. It would not be wise to take erroneous information to the police! The facts will be made clear to you soon. Wait. Do not act!

She read it and sat down heavily. "Well!"
Presently she rapped on the windowpane with

her ring. One of the guards appeared at the kitchen door. "Professor Burke came home last night, as you know," she said. "But I want you three men to keep that fact quiet."

"Sure. You need somebody around all day? The other two boys are getting kind of sleepy."

"I'll let you know. But you might take turns napping on the side porch." She emphasized the need for secrecy concerning the professor.

Just who, whe wondered, would have sufficient prestige—and know-how—to accomplish her object? Worriedly she dismissed one after another. She thought of the name of a man she did not know, who would be right. She looked in the book and dialed.

When the professor came down for breakfast, a car was leaving the driveway. He had a glimpse of a face.

"Morning, Bedelia! That looked like Marigold Macey."

"It was." Bedelia's large eyes were brilliant. "Sit down, Martin. And start your breakfast. I have news for you."

"News?"

"You're dead!" She showed him the letter.

He read rapidly. "Who sent it? How did it get here? Are the Sanders men still around?"

"The men are. Getting tired, too."

"The—Bedelia! I killed that man!"

"Maybe you did—and a good thing, too!"

He was horrified. "Not for anything on earth—

131

no matter how low—even a foreign agent—would I have—!"

"Martin! Collect yourself! Isn't it much more likely that he came to, tried to escape when he found he had been left behind, and they killed him?"

"But how could they confuse him with me? His hair was light—his skin very dark . . ."

"It's obvious from the letter that they *did* confuse him! Perhaps the men who killed him were unfamiliar with him—you—whoever. Disposed of the body hurriedly—in the sea—as the letter says. It looks like that to me."

He shuddered. "The unlucky devil . . . !"

"Good gracious, Martin, where is your sense of proportion? Don't you see what an opportunity this is?"

His mind worked jerkily. "Confession," he said slowly. "Yes—I can understand that. They could select a page here and there—and it would certainly look like a confession. In my own handwriting!"

"Please, Martin. Go on with your breakfast! Look at it from their point of view. They think they have murdered you. They know there will be an investigation, in any case. All the police—the Vellehomez police—will need a few pages from that account you wrote of the Maroon Gang—select pages, as you say—and a couple of witnesses to your 'suicide.' The Maroon Gang down there can supply the witnesses easily enough and hand-

132

writing experts will attest to the confession, so-called."

He stared at her.

"I phoned Marigold Macey an hour ago," she went on.

"What for?"

"Because I knew she'd come right over. I knew, furthermore, that she'd believe what I told her. Few would. Martin, there are—sometimes—really formidable disadvantages in a perfect reputation. And I knew she could get straight to her father—even if he had to be called out of court."

"Judge Macey? But—"

"He could determine, properly, who should be informed. That's important. The police? The F.B.I.? And not only that. He can persuade the top man to see you—so there won't. be any mistakes."

He waved his oatmeal spoon. "All right. What do we do meantime?"

"You just lie low. Don't show yourself. If anybody comes by—go upstairs and keep quiet."

Noon. One o'clock. Two.

Marigold neither returned nor reported back. No carload of police rushed to the verdure-clad gate of the house on West Cortez Circle. Calls to the Macey residence were not answered. The professor became alarmed.

Shortly after two o'clock, there was a brief, hard shower. The sun came out again. A scissors-grinder began to work his way down the street, calling his profession in a doleful voice and walking to each door in search of business.

"I won't wait any longer," the professor said, at last. "Something must have happened to Marigold!"

Bedelia was equally as worried. She heard footsteps at that moment, however, and peered through the window. "It's that scissor-grinder! You better duck." She went to the door.

The man was tall and dirty faced. He wore a leather apron. He held out some sample knives and scissors. "Sharpen anything, lady," he said. "Expert job. Low rates—"

"I don't want—"

He held the knives and scissors under her nose. Amidst them was a badge. Bedelia saw the letters, F.B.I. "Come in," she said. "I'll get together a few things, at that."

He entered the hall. His voice was low and quick. "There are at least two men skulking around outside."

Bedelia rapped on the window. "All right, Dusty. You can leave now. And thanks just infinitely. Remember. Tell nobody about any arrival here last night."

Dusty was weary but game. "Yes, Miss Ogilvy."

"Who was that?" the G-man asked.

"Just—friends. Watching. Now, I want better proof that you are who you say you are."

He glanced around the living room. "Phone?"

"In the kitchen."

"My name is Harmon. I'm the head of the local office. From what the Judge said, I decided to come, myself. From what his daughter said, I used that scissor-grinder gag. I haven't done anything like it for a long tme. But we thought the Maroon Gang might be covering the place. I've got men up and down the street. You call the office —and then we'll both talk." He grinned at her.

She smiled back, but she called. *Anybody,* she thought, *could have a G-man's badge.* Her call satisfied her. She faced him with relief. "I'm so glad it's over!"

He had, she thought, really handsome dark-blue eyes. His lips twitched. "Over? I suspect, Miss Oglivy, you've just started. Where is the professor?"

She looked at him and he could see tension return around her eyes, determination in her jaw. *Quite a dame,* he thought.

"Martin!" she called up the stairway.

He ran down the stairs. He was carrying the coat of the nameless man. She introduced them.

The G-man's eyes took in the coat, the lining-inside-the-lining, and the bills in their stitched compartments. They moved to the professor and his copper-stained face. "Suppose," he said, "you begin at the beginning—wherever that is. The Judge and his daughter were pretty lurid, but not too coherent. If it had been anybody else, I would have sent a psychiatrist out here."

The professor nodded. "I was lecturing about

135

civic corruption and crime—my last lecture class before vacation—" He broke off. "Good lord! It was only a little over a week ago! Seems years! Anyhow—"

The G-Man interrupted him an hour later to drive the scissor-grinding truck out of sight and to make a contact with his men. He came back and talked until it was dark.

"Professor Burke," he said as he was leaving, "it's up to you. We have no right to ask it. You already know the risk . . ." His amiable mouth straightened.

"I'll do it, naturally."

"See you, then. And thanks."

Professor Burke picked up the evening paper and went indoors. There was a smell of dinner in the air. He yelped.

"Something the matter, Martin?"

He rushed into the kitchen.

There were headlines on the front page:

MIAMI PROFESSOR SUICIDE AFTER CONFESSING UNDERWORLD LINK

Noted Psychologist Was Gem Smuggler

"Bedelia gave the black type only a glance. But she looked at the professor keenly. "Read it, Martin. I've got something on the stove I can't leave."

His voice shook slightly. "It's a special dispatch

136

to this paper," he said. " 'Vellehomez, Cuba, December 26. Martin Luther Burke, professor of socio-psychology at the University of Miami committed suicide here early today after writing a dramatic confession of his connections with the underworld. The professor, a leading authority in his field, and the author of *Ruminations of a Socio-Psychologist,* was seen by local fishermen to row out at dawn into the deep water off the harbor at Vellehomez, where he had been staying for the past twenty-four hours at a local inn. He seemed to meditate for a time, according to the witnesses, and then plunged overboard, leaving in his skiff the numbered, handwritten pages of his confession, many of which were blown into the sea and lost before the skiff was recovered. What was saved, leaves no doubt of his affiliations with the infamous Maroon Gang, a fact extremely shocking to his University associates. The body was not found.

" 'In the professor's room at the run-down hotel jewels valued at many thousands of dollars were found and these, together with references to "smuggling" in his extraordinary confession, have led the police to assume that the reason for his presence in Cuba was to bring the gems illegally into the U.S. His wallet—"

He said vehemently, "I didn't have a wallet!"

"They provided you with one!"

" '—contained cards to some of the more notorious gambling resorts in South Florida and Cuba, a souvenir blue chip, and a considerable sum of money. Handwriting experts, examining pages of the confession which were immediately flown to Miami by Cuban police officials say it is unquestionably the work of the late Professor Burke. Samples of his writing were supplied by the University.

" 'The professor's masquerade completely deceived his associates. When told of it on the phone by a Miami *Times* reporter, President Tolver of the University flatly refused to believe it and took it as some form of practical joke. "Burke," he insisted, "is a man above reproach." Professor Lothar MacFalkland, Burke's colleague in socio-psychology, a science in which the University hopes to develop a major department, took a different view of the matter, however.' "

Bedelia said, "M'm'm'm. I bet he did!"

The professor swore. It was the first time she had ever heard him use a real, ringing oath.

"Listen to this!" The newspaper shook in his hands. " 'According to MacFalkland, the late Professor Burke "suffered from a condition of over-repression and developed a dual personality from inner psychic pressures. Burke," said Dr. MacFalkland, who is a specialist in the field of personality, "is a typical bi-cerebral. This means he has two natures—one of which seems to be in control, while the other is actually in control. I have long perceived that the overperfection of his work at

138

the University has pointed to a blowup. I used constantly to urge him to get out more among people—to live a more normal life. I have been anticipating some news of this sort for a long."

"That fathead! That oaf! That overstuffed shirt!"

Bedelia made a sound like a giggle.

He read on: " 'Further developments in the fabulous case are expected momentarily. Cuban police are now searching for a handsome brunette who vanished from the hotel at Vellehomez. She is suspected of having brought the jewels into Cuba from South America and it is believed that her arrest may lead to the unmasking of the smuggling "ring" mentioned in the random pages of the professor's confession. These are now being studied by police of both countries.

" 'Professor Burke was thirty-three years old, a bachelor, and a New Englander by birth. He is survived by no close relatives. He was educated in the public schools of Massachusetts, Israel Putnam Teacher's College, where he graduated with honors, and Harvard. He taught for some time in the University of New Jersey. During the war he served as a foreign language expert attached to the 118th Training Service Corps. He has been a full professor at the University of Miami for the past three years. Pictures on page 4.' "

He turned to page four and looked at a photograph of himself—enlarged from a panoramic

139

picture of the faculty—a photograph of President Tolver, and one of MacFalkland. He hurled the paper on the table. "The imbecile!"

He stalked around the kitchen. "Wilser—or one of them—must have picked out pages of my account that didn't mention the Maroon Gang very definitely—pages that made it sound as if . . . !" He shrugged. "I did use phrases like, 'According to my knowledge—' and, 'the inside truth is'— and I suppose it would seem like a confession— if you only had a few pages carefully chosen—"

"Dinner," she said, "is just about ready."

"I am going to punch that MacFalkland square on the nose! Bi-cerebral, my eye! There is no such term! A cheap play for newspaper publicity! Tampering with science!" He sat down then, with a sort of groan. "Bedelia, do you realize this thing will follow me all my life? Do you realize I'll be marked! Academically ruined!"

"I wouldn't worry about that now, Martin. You have problems that are much more immediate."

Seventeen:

THE ENSUING days were busy ones for the professor.

He spent them with the F.B.I.

His name—for this purpose—was Mr. Skeat. It proved that Professor Burke, in his school years, had been called "Skeet"—for "Skeeter"—a name which referred to his then markedly small size. It also proved that he still responded, even from the most absent-minded reverie, to "Skeet." This became "Mr. Skeat."

The professor was now adorned with horn-rimmed glasses which had tinted lenses. His hair had been cut very short and bleached to a light hue. As the iodine faded from his skin, it was replaced by a scientific colorant. Flamboyant sports clothes were purchased for him—clothes typical of those worn by Florida tourists. The synthetic Mr. Skeat registered then at a downtown hotel in Miami: the Palm Plaza.

Bedelia and her premises were kept under constant, covert surveillance. She objected; but Harmon did not agree that she was "old enough to take care of herself."

"Mr. Skeat"—Mr. Ralph Skeat, of Newark

New Jersey—was a very plausible hotel guest and tourist. He went to the races. He attended the Orange Bowl Game. He visited the night clubs nearly every evening. Sometimes he was accompanied by a gentleman—sometimes by a lady.

He was engaged in a comparatively simple enterprise. He had given a veritable encyclopaedia of fresh information to the F.B.I. But the personnel of the Maroon Gang—especially in its comparatively new smuggling activities—was not all known to the government agents. The connections between French Paul and the other leading figures in the Gang were plain—as the professor's investigations had shown—but that fact did not constitute legal evidence. "Mr. Skeat" was therefore visiting those places where gang members known to him might appear.

In the course of this research, the professor saw his first prize fights, wrestling matches and the interiors of dozens of night clubs, cabarets, bistros and dives. His work was not without result. He identified "Chuck" in one of the late night spots and he pointed out the man known as The Foot at the race track.

Chuck and The Foot, thereafter had the F.B.I. on their heels by day and by night, though they did not know it.

The professor was also taken on several daylight flights over the lakes and lagoons of the flat, marshy wilderness that is South Florida. He and his pilot searched for a lake that would have the necessary qualifications: water enough for a plane, a grassy shore line, a background of trees—probably cypresses—a rough connecting road, and possibly, although not necessarily, a small dock. It turned out that there were dozens of sites which more or less satisfied these requirements. Professor Burke did not succeed in locating the one where he and the three aliens had been landed.

From scraps of information gleaned cautiously in Cuba, the F.B.I. learned fairly clearly how the nameless man had been mistaken for the professor, how he had tried to escape, how he had been killed and disposed of. This knowledge was very comforting to the professor, who feared his two blows with the rusty monkey wrench had killed the man.

It was thus certain that the Maroon Gang and even the police of Miami and of Cuba were convinced the professor was dead. Bedelia's apparent obedience of the terms of the anonymous letter substantiated the conviction. She joined those who discussed the professor's sinister *alter ego*. And such is the mixed nature of South Florida society that, quite probably, word went back to the Maroon Gang that Bedelia Ogilvy was no longer a peril to their activities—that she, too, believed in the professor's sins and his suicide.

New Year's Eve was calm. That night, the *Mary Fifth* put out to see with a gay party aboard. But there were no ship-to-shore messages. Nothing untoward happened in Vellehomez. The radar of a Coast Guard vessel did, it is true, pick up an unidentified plane flying north from Cuba—a plane that was inaudible at a range in which it should have been heard. But neither the place of take-off nor of landing was ascertained.

An important fact was established, however: the Maroon Gang had begun smuggling again. French Paul evidently felt that his rapid calculations and activities had ended all suspicions and inquiries concerning the professor. Even the newspapers—excepting for one nationally circulated Sunday supplement—had exhausted the saga of the social scientist who "turned against society." The Sunday magazine, however, began publication of a series of articles by MacFalkland, called, "The Psychology of America's Slickest Criminal—as told by One Who Knew Him."

Eighteen:

Two NIGHTS after New Year's Professor Burke was recognized. His duties had taken him back to the Club Egret. As "Mr. Skeat," he had been there on several occasions. He had caught glimpses of Miss Maxson and yearned to speak with her. It had been out of the question.

This evening, he went out to dinner alone. Harmon said that one of his men—Cleves, from Tacoma, Washington, whom the professor now knew—would join him later. "Mr. Skeat" saw nobody save the night club habitués. He had finished his dinner and was smoking a cigarette—another addition to his disguise and one he, as a pipe-and-cigar-smoker, did not enjoy—when the lights went down and the same comedian appeared, with a joke that dated back to a situation in a comedy by Terence.

The professor was listening rather idly when a girl's voice said, "Your slip's showing, darling."

Connie Maxson was standing in the luminous gloom.

He pretended not to know she had spoken to him.

"May I sit? After all—I'm a sort of hostess."

145

He beckoned with his cigarette. He did not rise. He glanced at the nearer tables. Nobody was interested.

She laughed softly. "What magnificent publicity you've been getting!"

"How did you—?"

She leaned forward and spoke quietly. "You dope! I've been watching for you for over a week!"

"Watching for me! "I'm—dead."

Connie chuckled. "You don't look it. You look pretty sporty."

"What gave me away?"

"Remember the night your dear old Bedelia asked for protection—and Bill sent it? Well—naturally Dusty and the boys told Bill that you'd made it back. Nobody else. And naturally Bill told me. And nobody else. So we knew you were somewhere, and we expected you'd be doing—what you evidently are. Acting as eyes for—people. And looking quite different. When you came in and took this table by the wall, tonight, I began to think it was you. And when you didn't laugh at Benny's joke, just now, I took a better look. The spotlight shows up your profile. And a girl gets to know the profiles of the men she's kissed."

"I've wanted to see your uncle. To thank him. To ask him to forgive me for spreading around so much of the confidential information he gave me. I was careful—always—to shield him."

Connie nodded her high-piled, wheat-colored

146

hair. "He noticed it. And appreciates it. How's it going?"

"So-so."

"I better not stay long."

"No," he said wistfully.

"I suppose you know how Bill will feel if you pull off what you must be trying?"

"Sore at me, I guess. I spilled a lot of beans."

"Sore at you!" Her voice dropped still farther and she leaned closer to him. He could smell the perfume. He was used to such perfumes, now. "Bill's having a tough time. It's a big season. But those people are muscling in. They have some sort of an inside track Bill can't figure. He's afraid he's going to have to close up. He won't cut them in—and that's all there is to that." She rose, patting his hand. "It was nice seeing you. And don't worry. I doubt if anybody else on earth—including your own best friend—would realize."

She left and he felt lonely. He found his imagination introducing her: "This is Mrs. Burke." She would be a sensational professor's wife. But he would be a sensational professor—too sensational. Even granted that this interminable impersonation ended, that everything ended well, his career would be a wreck. Who would want, on a dignified faculty, such a character as he had become—not just by newspaper allegation, but in fact?

He smoked a cigarette and watched the tango act.

Her penetration of his disguise made him

147

vaguely uneasy. It was true that she had known he was alive. True that she had been expecting him to appear in a disguise of some sort. But he had come to think of his changed appearance as impenetrable. Chuck, for example, had looked straight at him and shown no sign whatever of recognition.

He put out his cigarette, paid his check, and strolled into the gambling room. He bought a few two-dollar chips and took a stance at a roulette table which gave him a view of the dice tables, too. Harmon had told him that men of the sort for whom he was searching would be more likely to shoot dice than to play roulette.

He began winning. He had been uncommonly lucky in the occasional gambling he had done during his undercover travels through the night-time world of Greater Miami and of Broward County, to the north. Harmon had wanted to pay all his expenses—with government funds. The professor had insisted on using his own money— the eight hundred dollars from his first night's try at roulette. There was, in this process, an irony that amused him: the world of gambling, corruption and vice, the world about which he had once so innocently lectured, was paying for an investigation of itself.

It was about ten when the man entered the gambling room. He knew a lot of people, waved at them, stopped to chat. He congratulated one or two winners over their heaps of chips and frowned with pleasant sympathy at those who complained of bad luck. His hair was as slick and shiny as the fender of a new black car. The comparison came to mind because the man made the professor think of cars.

It was Solo. The man who, twice, had picked up loads of "passengers" from the silent plane.

The professor went on playing. Among the people to whom Solo had spoken was a middle-aged woman in a scarlet evening dress who was recklessly distributing chips on the numbered geometry of the table. He moved, presently, to her side. She had looked, several times, at the stalwart back of Solo, who was now watching one of the dice games. An overweight female, flushed from too many cocktails, and talkative—a type with which the professor had become familiar.

When he approached, she said, "Welcome, partner!"

He waited until she stole another look at Solo. The croupier was calling the spin.

"Handsome egg."

The woman turned. Her eyes glittered over her puffy cheeks. "You said something!"

"Who is he?"

"The Tip? He's the assistant manager of this joint." She leaned to place a chip and turned to watch the little ivory ball dance in its hypnotic vortex.

The professor felt coldness enter his veins. *The Tip.* "I know a man," Chuck had said, while the plane winged toward Cuba, "who only uses the tip of his knife." And Chuck had demonstrated.

The woman had just said, furthermore, "He's the assistant manager of this joint." That meant —if it were true—that Double-O had an associate who also belonged to the Maroon Gang. He thought of Connie's words: "They have some kind of an inside track that Bill can't figure."

They did have—unless . . .

The woman nudged him. "What's the matter? Can't you dream up a number?" He started and put a chip on six.

Unless Mr. Sanders and his niece were subtler than he thought. Subtler and—something else. Unless Mr. Sanders was *still* associated with the Maroon Gang. He had once worked for them. Could it be that he belonged? That, knowing an intense, secret investigation of the Maroon Gang was being made, he hoped the field would soon be cleared of them, and open to himself?

It was possible.

That was the trouble. It was possible. And it was not only possible, but it sounded very much like any of fifty schemes, stratagems and double crosses with which Mr. Sanders himself had filled in the sickening history of the Maroon Gang. He and French Paul could be feigned antagonists, but actual associates. Yet Double-O could be planning not to warn French Paul and his immediate associates but to let the law take them. In order to clean up afterward.

150

Gangsters—gamblers—criminals, the professor thought bitterly.

The Tip—Solo—whatever his name was—may have felt the stare that was boring into his back. He may have tired of watching the dice roll. He turned quickly. His eyes met those of "Mr. Skeat."

And, in the new dubiety about his incognito, the professor's eyes did the wrong things. They tried to look back casually; but they faltered and showed self-consciousness.

The Tip inspected the professor for a moment —in the way of a man who remembers a face and cannot place it. Then he shrugged a little and turned to make a laughing comment to one of the men at the table. Soon afterward he sauntered from the room. The professor went on playing, automatically. His mind seethed.

It was his duty to go quickly, unobtrusively, to a phone and call a certin number. Not Headquarters, but a private house. It was his duty to invite the woman who would answer to join him later—at another place. He would also tell her where he was. She would decline and he would hang up. An F.B.I. agent would appear shortly— and thenceforward the third man to be identified by "Mr. Skeat" would be relentlessly pursued, checked, shadowed and investigated.

That was his duty.

If Double-O did not know his assistant manager was a member of the Maroon Gang, Connie's words about the "inside track" were now clear—and Double-O had a very treacherous employee. He should be told.

That, in such a case, was also an obligation: Professor Burke felt his debt to the gambler intensely.

But if Double-O *knew who The Tip was* . . . ?

The dangers of that situation were too numerous and varied for quick reckoning. Not the least of them would be his own danger at this moment. At every moment from now on.

Nineteen:

THE TIP left the room with a sense of frustration. He had a memory for faces and he had seen that face. He had seen that face and, he vaguely felt, hated or feared it. Light had been reflected up into it from the green baize and the light had filtered down upon it from overhead. He had seen that face before—in a funny light.

He stood in the foyer. The dance band was playing. Dinner was over for most of them, but not drinking. The bar was crowded. Big night for Double-O. The Tip moved up beside one of the men in tuxedos who seemed to live in that foyer, close to the curtained entrance of the gambling room.

"Guy in there at the cheap table, Al. Tinted specs. Light hair—crew-cut—dark complexion—medium size. Who is he?"

Al went through the curtain and came back shortly. "Fellow named Ralph Skeat. Been around here a little."

"For how long?"

"Last ten days or so."

"Where from?"

"Don't know. Tourist. Never saw him, other years. There's millions like him, Tip."

153

The Tip walked out on the porch. The doorman and the parking attendants spoke deferentially.

He went down the broad steps. "Think I'll take a breather. Off my feed. Nice night."

They said it was a nice night.

The Tip walked toward Collins Avenue. He was thinking. Maybe it wasn't important. But he disliked not to know a face—especially when his related sensations were of alarm and hatred. On the sea side of Collins Avenue, near the Club Egret, was a vacant lot. A path led through it and The Tip followed the path to the edge of the sea. The shore at this point curved out a short distance, displaying the long arc of neon-flaming hotels down Miami Beach to his right and the spectacular new hotels at his left, to the north.

It was another calm evening. He reflected on the meaning of that fact.

Who in hell was the guy?

He lingered, staring over the starlit sea, recognition barely eluding him. Somewhere, a fish splashed.

"Great—!" he whispered shakily.

"Mr. Skeat" cashed his chips.

If the most dismal of his theories was fact, it might not even be safe to use a phone in the Club Egret. Double-O might have them tapped. The idea seemed ridiculous.

It seemed so ridiculous that he began to feel— not to think logically—that if he could have been so mistaken about Connie and Double-O there was no use trying to understand humanity, to live, to believe, to work for anything.

He went to the foyer. He addressed one of the men there. "Is Miss Maxson still around?"

"You know her, Mr. Skeat?"

"Slightly. She's talked with me a little."

"She might be."

The professor offered the man a twenty-dollar bill. "Would you see? And if she's here, ask her if she'll have a drink with me?"

The man was going to refuse the bill. When he saw its denomination, he changed his mind. "Thanks."

He came back soon. "She says, go to the bar."

Connie leaned over her drink.

"You shouldn't have asked for me!"

"Can you get out of here for a while?"

"What's the matter?"

"It's important! The man you call The Tip also works for—" he whispered—"French Paul."

"I don't believe it!" Her violence reassured him. Her blue eyes were panicky. "I'll get a hat."

She went. Minutes passed.

She came back wearing a hat.

The professor escorted her to the door. When it closed, the warmth of the evening enveloped them and the dance music became only a drum pulse. He gave the doorman his check. His rented car was brought around.

He went slowly among pretty, pastel-colored

155

houses. He told her what he knew about The Tip.

Once, she said, "He drove for them on Christmas Eve and Christmas Night? That could be. The Club was closed. The raid!" She laughed without pleasure. "You ought to remember."

"I do."

"We didn't open till two days later. There were repairs for one thing. They made a mess of the office—those cops—looking for the money that you and I had."

"Connie! I've got to take you back, now! I took a terrible chance—as it is. For a moment, I was afraid . . ."

"*That we knew!*"

He said desperately. "I've got so I hardly trust myself."

"Oh—Martin!"

Another of her kisses began.

He did not interrupt the kiss. But, when she let go of him, he said, "I have work to do."

"I know. Please be careful." She sighed unevenly. "All my life, Martin, I'll remember you. *You're something!*"

He drove back toward the low, white building where the people danced and the little white ball danced, too.

The Tip had returned—his face so pale that the doorman had said he surely must be off his feed. He had looked for "Mr. Skeat" and learned of his departure with Connie.

He put in a very private phone call.

156

When he came from the booth, he saw Connie vanishing through the rear door of the barroom.

He rushed to the front entry.

"Mr. Skeat" was just driving away. He got the number of the license. Then he ran to the parking yard for his own car.

In a drugstore, many blocks down Collins Avenue, the professor dialed a number and anxiously watched the street outside. His car was parked where he could see it.

"Harmon," he said into the phone. He added a little more.

"I was just leaving," Harmon said hurriedly. "They're working tonight; we think."

"Look! I'm on Collins—phone booth—first drug store below the Egret. Double-O's general factotum—The Tip—"

"I know him."

"—is also Solo, the driver of—"

An explosive, "No!" came over the wire.

"Right! I've told Miss Maxson. She has told Double-O. I think The Tip recognized me—"

"Recognized you!"

The professor's voice changed, but was still quite steady. "Harmon! *He recognized me, all right. He just drove by and gave my car the once-over!"*

"Listen, Professor! This is the sort of thing I was afraid of! I can't get to you or send a man to you! Can he see you from the street?"

"When I come out—sure."

"He'll shoot."

"But there might be a back door, too."

The G-man talked fast. "Okay. Use it. Or stay inside there. Do the best you can. If you try moving, Burke—hide. Don't go near Bedelia's. Don't go back to the hotel. Go—I've got it! Go to Judge Macey's place—"

"Macey's?"

"I'll send them word. I can't hang on any longer, Burke. Thanks. Thanks for everything. Good luck!"

Professor Burke opened the phone booth door. He peered again. The Tip had double-parked and was waiting.

"Is there a back way out of this place?"

The drug clerk looked at him. "What for?"

"There's a man out there I don't want to meet."

The druggist stared a moment longer—at direct, steady eyes. "Okay, bud. Turn left."

He passed shelves of bottles, entered a room stacked with cartons, and he saw the door. It led to a narrow walk.

He peered around the corner of the building.

The Tip was leaving his car. He moved toward the store—his right hand inside his jacket.

The professor waited an instant. He heard the automatic door-closer hiss. He ran across the walk. As he had expected, The Tip's motor was running.

He did not drive slowly—this time.

Twenty:

THE CAR went like a leaf in a wind tunnel. Even so, before the professor came to the first turn in Collins Avenue, he saw headlights twist from the curb. His car. The Tip would be frantic. A dead man had come back from the grave—a man who knew him in both identities. The Tip's reaction was simple: *get that man as soon as possible.*

Collins Avenue curved. There was a red light. The professor howled his brakes and went through the light. He made an S-turn. Ahead was a wide, straight stretch. He pressed on the horn-rim and followed its blast. When he had another opportunity, he looked in his mirror. The Tip was gaining.

Collins Avenue turned left at the end of that stretch, but the professor went straight ahead on Indian Creek Drive. He got around a truck and in front of a convertible, came out again on Collins, and looked back. The pursuing car was still closer. Down the avenue, beside the Roney-Plaza Hotel— pink and tremendous in the brilliance of Twenty-third Street—traffic waited in a solid huddle for the light to change. He stopped and jumped out, abandoning the car in the midst of many others. He ducked through them and ran across a parking yard. He heard The Tip's brakes scream.

In front of him was the blind pocket of water called Lake Surprise, a salt pond connected with Indian Creek and the canals. Sightseeing boats were tied up there. A high, curved bridge spanned the backwater. A man with a megaphone was still barking a late ride. Small private craft lay at numerous little docks; around one were several water bicycles. People were pedaling them about on the lake. The professor snatched bills from his pocket, pressed five dollars into the hand of the water-bike attendant, jumped onto one, and churned furiously toward the canal—and comparative dark.

A car on the shore behind him backfired. A fast bee buzzed past the professor. A tiny wind fanned his cheek.

The Tip was shooting.

Ahead, the waters were contained between cement banks over which bushes hung. He pedaled with all his might. There was another report. The bullet ripped his jacket. He went around the first of the overhanging shrubs.

On the street behind him came the faint sounds of people yelling. He drove the pontooned craft down the dark canal and saw another bridge ahead. He scrambled ashore, setting the water-cycle adrift. He ran across Dade Boulevard and into the golf course, behind the fire house. He caught his breath.

A large, white hotel stood on the other side of the golf course. He reconnoitered it from behind a clump of oleanders. People on the street. Cars coming and going. A cab driver reading a comic book.

The Tip had probably eluded any chase that might have started and was doubtless hunting again. Possibly he had called the mansion on the Bayfront and reported to French Paul. Perhaps the Maroon Gang was getting the word even now —and starting from houses, night clubs, gambling places, bookie joints and other regions to hunt in the city for a man with light hair, crew-cut, and a dark complexion.

The professor walked up to the cab. "Want to go over to the Gables," he said. "In kind of a hurry."

He got out near the center of Coral Gables. They might expect him to head for Bedelia's. And he wanted to walk, wanted to be certain, before he approached the Macey house, that no one was following.

He came up to it from the rear. Lights were burning. He entered the hedged garden and sat for minutes in the chair where Marigold had once sat beside him. He breathed and listened. There had been no one—all the way. He knocked on the back door.

The kitchen light went on. Marigold was wearing her hair down. She had on a housecoat— white and gold. She peered through the glass and unlocked the door. "I've been practically out of my mind! Mr. Harmon called over an hour ago and I expected you right away!"

He came in. "Better pull the blinds."

She stared. "Good heavens! Look at you!"

"Where's your father?"

"Out. He and mother went to Fort Myers to visit friends this afternoon. And Steve's out, too—with his girl. That usually means four A.M. So I've got you in my clutches."

He said, "Thank the lord!"

She was shaking. "What happened? Bedelia has given us an idea of what you were working on. Come in the den and tell me. It's got Venetian blinds and draperies you can pull. Mr. Harmon told me to keep you out of sight—and above everything else, to keep you. What tore your coat?"

He followed her through a hallway and into the judge's den. She repeated her last question.

"Bullet," he said.

He was not prepared to have her throw her arms around him and kiss him. "Oh, Martin! You're—all right?"

It made, he thought, two girls and two major kisses for the evening. A double life—with two women in it. He gathered her long, curly hair in his right hand, pulled her head back so that her face was turned up, and kissed her again.

"I'm all right. The guy missed."

"Who was it?"

He sat down in the judge's leather easy chair. "Look, Marigold. For Heaven's sake stop asking me things! I *think* I've done everything I could. I let Harmon know. I told Connie."

"Connie who? Martin—is that the blonde you were necking a few days ago at the Bombay Roy-ale? Jim Ellis and Nancy Beatty saw you. It was all over the campus the next morning."

His eyes twinkled. "A small matter—in view of subsequent findings! I am a criminal, a gangster, a jewel smuggler—not to mention dead by my own hand!"

"I was jealous," she said simply. "Martin, Would you like coffee?"

Twenty-one:

HE LIGHTED one of the judge's cigars and watched blue smoke spiral toward the ceiling. Harmon would have gone to wherever he was going. The place, he silently hoped, where the plane would land. Sanders would have made whatever provision he felt necessary concerning The Tip. But it was not likely The Tip would return to the Club Egret. Not ever.

He was out of it. After tonight, his incognito would be worthless. He could emerge from it. Resign from the University, he thought somberly. Make a last call on MacFalkland. Find another position, if he could.

Marigold came with a tray. Light brown hair lying softly on her gold and white shoulders. She poured coffee. He watched her achingly. In a few days, he'd be on his way. Never see her again. Never see Connie again. There was a French folk song:

> *Oh, les fraise et les framboises,*
> *Les vins que nous avons bu,*
> *Et les belles villageoise,*
> *Nous ne les verrons plus.*

And the pretty village girls, we'll never see them again. It was supposed to be a gay song.

She poured coffee and put the cup on a table beside him. "Can I sit in your lap?"

"No!"

"Why not, Martin? The other day—when you stepped on Dad's pineapples—I thought—"

"That, Marigold, was because you are beautiful and I used to be a professor in good standing—with a lot of admiration for you and a certain amount of curiosity."

"Was it the limit of your curiosity?"

He shook his head. "I'm somebody else, now, Marigold. I don't even know who."

"That—*Connie!*"

"Connie's a wonderful girl, too. But I'm—phychologically a little dated for you modern girls. I was brought up to be old-fashioned."

"Don't you know that a great many modern girls act modern just to get a chance to become old-fashioned?"

"Do they?" He smoked and smiled and finally shook his head. "You sit down over there, Marigold, and let me be. I want to think. Harmon—out in the Glades—down in the Keys. A plane flying —a grim business that's got to stop."

"Bedelia told me. It's—"

"Inhuman!" He flicked ashes into his saucer. "Such a profound amount of imagination and skill in the thing! Right now—out somewhere on the

165

Gulf Stream—there's a boat called the *Mary Fifth* —" he broke off.

"Doing what?"

He did not hear her. His mind had gone back to the plane cabin—to the feel of sash wieghts wired on his handcuffs—to Chuck's voice: "On the nights we fly, maybe the *Mary Fifth*—that's a Miami boat—goes out fishing."

He had told the F.B.I. that it *was* the *Mary Fifth*—that the *Mary Fifth* always went out, when they flew. Suppose Chuck had meant that maybe, at times, it was *some other boat?*

"Where's the phone?"

"Mr. Harmon said you were just to sit here!"

It was one thirty but he dialed the Fishing Pier. The phone rang, rang, rang on and on. Finally a disgruntled voice said, "Yeah?"

"Is the *Mary Fifth* there?"

"This is a hell of a time to call about a charter! I'm the mate on the *Binney*—and you woke me up—"

"Is she there?"

"Yeah—she's here and locked up tight and the crew gone home hours ago. Gimme your name— and I'll leave a note for them to call in the morning."

He dialed another number.

"Federal Bureau of Investigation."

"This is Mr. Skeat."

"Wilson speaking."

"Is it possible to reach Harmon?"

"No, Professor. What's up?"

"The *Mary Fifth* didn't go out tonight."

"We know that. They're probably operating without her." Wilson's voice was amiable. "Make it that much easier for Harmon and the rest."

"They might have used another boat."

"Yeah? Did you mention it?"

"I just thought of it."

Wilson swore. "Harmon overlooked it."

"He didn't overlook it, man! I told him there was just one boat. The rest of my information was right so we took that statement for granted, too."

"I don't know how we—at this point—"

"Can you find out from the Miami Marine Operator what boats, if any, are outside tonight? Getting calls?"

"Sure!"

"Ring me here. You know where I am?"

"Macey's house. Oke."

He waited tensely. The phone rang within three minutes.

"Wilson, here. Look. Marine calls have been pretty slow tonight. One to Cat Cay. A houseboat named the *Spanish Galleon* is out with a party up around the Haulover some place. They had a long talk, half an hour ago. A lot of stuff about hanging a shark and fighting it and planning to beach it."

"Beach it?"

"That's what the operator said. *Good lord!*"

"You'll need men all along there, then!" The professor spoke fast. "There's that empty stretch between the Haulover and Golden Beach."

"Professor—we haven't got one man left."

"Police."

"We've got fifteen names on the list. How long will it take one wrong guy to find out—if the cops start getting up a posse now?"

"Certainly you could pick your men . . ."

"I can try. Harmon will probably shoot himself if the whole gang's working on a bum lead!"

The professor hung up. "You got a car, Marigold?"

Her eyes were vivid. "In two seconds, I'll change!"

"We haven't two seconds—and I'm going alone."

"Unless I can go with you, I won't be able to find the key."

He looked at her for a long, thoughtful moment.

"Get your clothes. Change in the car."

She ran upstairs and ran back in seconds. She led the way to the garage.

Coral Gables unwound behind them. They cut from the Tamiami Trail to Twenty-seventh Avenue. It was wide, empty, and fast. He ran clear to Seventy-ninth—a causeway street—and within twenty minutes he was moving north in Miami Beach. At the bridge over the waters which make an island of Miami Beach, gasoline lights burned and a score of diligent net-casters stared concentratedly into the swift, slick tide below.

He drove smoothly up the road. The sea was a dozen feet below them and not many yards away. Here and there, a beach fire glowed. A few cars were parked on the land side; it was a favorite rendezvous for people who weren't ready to go home yet. For young people, especially.

The professor turned off the road and switched out his lights. "If the houseboat is operating off the Haulover, it should be somewhere yonder." He pointed to the sea, a murmuring darkness that extended to a final nothing, above which stars shone.

"What do we do now?"

He looked at her in the beam of a slowly approaching car. She had changed to a dark dress—and pinned up her hair—somehow, in the rocking, bumping seat. The car passed and went on. "Just watch," he said. "If they intend to beach a shark, they'd do it here."

"Why?"

"Too many hotels and people—too much doing—below here. Above here, there's another long stretch where people live." He opened the door. "We'll go out on the road and patrol a bit."

They crossed the highway. Small waves spilled and hissed on the sand. Far to the north, city lights glowed. To the south were the gas lanterns of the bridge-anglers. In between was a mile and a half, or perhaps two miles, of beach, dunes, underbrush, and road. Not a house or a building.

"Wouldn't it be better," she asked, after they had walked for several minutes, "if we split up? If I patrolled in one direction and you in the other?"

"Do you think it's a good idea for a girl to be walking around in this place alone?"

"It would just double our chances of seeing anything. What happens, if we do see anything?"

"We run for the car, and wait, and follow them."

She looked at him a moment. "Okay. You go north. I'll go toward the bridge and come back. Meet here."

Twenty-two:

HE WALKED at the edge of the road. Every few rods he stopped and strained his eyes out toward the sea. In the remote distance, Fowey Rock periodically displayed a wand, white flare and channel markers winked in the oblivion between. He had long since lost sight of Marigold—a dwindling figure, visible for a while in the sudden illumination of the cars that passed her. There were not many.

They passed him, too. In one of them, he thought he saw uniformed police, but he was not sure. He went to the end of his beat where habitation began again. He walked back more swiftly, looking less often at the sea and worrying about the girl. She was waiting for him opposite the car.

"See anything?" They said the same thing at the same time—and laughed.

"It's probably foolish . . ." he said. "The information from the Marine Operator was suggestive—that's all."

"Let's go again."

She had walked about halfway back from the Haulover bridge when she heard the launch. She moved from the road down to the beach, and found a sea lavender behind which she could hide. The motor was not running fast—idling, rather. It came toward the shore very slowly. She could not see it. But she thought she had better get the professor. She expected that she would have to go the full length of the uninhabited beach. But she did not.

He had decided it was too great a risk for her to be there, alone, and turned back before reaching the end of his route. They met a few hundred yards north of her car. Panting, she told him.

He led her back to the car. He started the motor but he did not turn on his lights. He drove up over the shoulder and headed south, going slowly. No one approached from either direction.

"It was about here," she said.

He turned from the pavement and parked.

Together, they went down to the beach. They squatted behind the sea lavender.

The motor was plainly audible. He thought he could hear voices out on the dark water.

"It's much nearer!" she whispered.

"I think I can see it. Not quite straight out. A little to the left. A white blur—"

"It is!"

"Coming in gradually."

Behind them, on the road, a large sedan approached—so slowly that he pulled her around to the ocean side of the bush to keep from being noticed. The car went beyond them for perhaps a city block and stopped. It backed into one of the parking places and its lights died out.

"More people necking," she whispered. "Lucky them!"

He murmured, "Maybe."

The white blur became boat-shaped. Voices above its engine sounded cheerful and urgent. *Was it possible . . . ?*

It was not a large boat. But he made out many heads silhouetted against the less dark water. A considerable splashing accompanied the slow progress toward shore.

One voice, louder than the rest, came to their ears: "Stay with it, Doc! You only got a few more feet to go!"

More babble. More splashes. The launch was such a craft as a good-sized, well-appointed houseboat might carry in her davits—for fishing, or for emergencies. And now the professor could see a rod bent in her stern.

The conversation reported by the Miami Marine Operator had not been bogus. Somebody on the *Spanish Galleon* off Bakers Haulover, had actually hooked a big shark, a couple of hours before and, lacking the equipment for gaffing such a fish, was beaching it. The big sedan behind them was as innocent as the rest of the random traffic.

The professor jeered at himself.

He had entertained a slight suspicion. On the strength of it, he had roused the F.B.I. He had

173

severely worried Wilson. He had, perhaps, sent others out on a false errand.

He should have left the affairs of that night to men who knew their business.

"What did you say?" she whispered.

"I was swearing."

"That's what I thought." She reached for his hand. "Never mind! It was a quite a buzz—while it lasted! Look! They're getting out in the water. The boat's aground. Let's stay and see what they caught. Nothing, I bet, but an old hammerhead. Maybe even just a big nurse shark."

"Wait a minute!" His whisper was sharp.

He had seen something that no fisherman would do: the man with the bent rod had tossed it into the sea. And the people were not encouraging an "angler" any longer. They were getting out of the launch swiftly, silently, and wading toward the beach. Half a dozen men—and two women. One of the men was very fat.

"They *weren't* fishing!" Her voice was low and tense.

He shook his head.

"Then they *are* . . . !"

He nodded and pulled her down behind the bush on the cool sand.

The fat man waited until the last person had stepped out of the water. "Rudolph!" he called loudly. The lights of the big sedan turned on.

The people on the beach were not directly in the rays, but they were near enough to be visible, now.

174

The professor bit hard on his lower lip. French Paul—Wilser—and some strangers. Strangers who had doubtless just arrived, by a very quiet plane, from Cuba. French Paul either knew or had guessed that every agent in South Florida was concentrated on the Keys and in the Everglades. So he had boldy brought the travelers ashore almost on Miami Beach itself, superintending the maneuver personally—as he had on one other occasion the professor knew of.

The eight people started to scramble up on the road.

"Stand right where you are everybody! Hands up!"

The hard voice had not finished when a pistol cracked in the hand of the fat Alsatian. Wilser knelt and began firing. The others scattered, running back along the beach. From the road came the blast of automatic guns. A woman screamed. Bullets burned above the heads of the two people lying behind the bush. Feet pounded on the road. Car lights blazed up and down the beach.

"Stand still! Everybody!"

The shots ceased. The whole beach above was well illuminated. The sand below was shaded by dunes.

Police were rounding up the men and the two women. "This way! Bring 'em up this way," a voice commanded.

Weeds whispered close beside the girl and the man. The professor rolled over on his back. He

175

wanted to see—but he did not want to stand up suddenly and be shot at.

French Paul was creeping through the brush, in the shadow of the steep slope beside the road. He was out of sight and he would soon be far enough out of range to run. Or to wade into the calm sea and swim. A man like French Paul could probably swim a long distance.

"Drop your gun, Paul," the professor said sharply.

Paul turned toward the tangle—staring. The professor kicked up at the man's arm with all his might.

The gun flew. Paul lunged. Marigold yelled.

Police rushed toward them . . .

The morning paper displayed a banner headline:

FBI SMASHES MAROON GANG

Prof. Burke, Thought Dead, Credited for Coup
Leaders Jailed
Alien-Smuggling Ring Bared

EXTRA!

There were similar headlines throughout the day in the nation's press.

The radio networks talked breathlessly about it.

Harmon read the headlines in his office. He had not slept and his eyes revealed the fact. But he did not seem interested in going to bed. It was the day of his life.

At Bog Key, the night before, he and his men had intercepted a second plane—and its crew of two: Chuck and Johnny. G-men, in a dozen cities, had arrested more than a hundred members of the Maroon Gang and people associated with them. Thirty-eight persons had been arrested in Cuba.

When Harmon had rushed anxiously back to Miami, he had found French Paul, as well as the others on board the *Spanish Galleon* and her launch, in the custody of the police. Professor Burke and Marigold Macey were waiting for him —the professor with a suggestion which led to the predawn capture of The Tip. It was a clean sweep.

Reporters crowded around the desk of the G-man. "How good," they asked, "is your case?"

Harmon laughed. "While Burke was going around as 'Mr. Skeat' we had time to make it watertight. And listen, fellows. You haven't even started to give Burke the credit he deserves." The G-man tapped the newspaper on his desk . . .

Mrs. MacFalkland nervously woke her husband. "There's some rather disquieting news in the paper, dear . . ."

He muttered and opened his eyes. "Those Russians!"

"Nothing like that." In spite of her anxiety, she concealed a sudden grimace. It might have been a smile. Perhaps she enjoyed the prospect of seeing—just once—the complete discomfiture of her too-positive husband. "It turns out that Professor Burke isn't dead."

"Isn't dead!" He grabbed the paper. Horror filled his eyes . . .

Connie heard it on the radio while she was eating breakfast. She drove to the Bombay Royale. Double-O was wearing a red dressing gown with a monogram of two linked zeroes on its pocket. He grinned at her and sent his butler for another coffee cup.

"What happened?" the girl asked feverishly.

"Most of it's in the papers. This edition came out too early to mention The Tip."

"They got him?"

"Burke suggested last night to Harmon that I could tell them where The Tip might hide. I did. I went down to headquarters about four o'clock and stayed a while. Identifying a couple of miscellaneous clucks the G-men didn't know."

"The professor and that girl could have been killed!"

Double-O walked to the window. "Yeah."

"The police—and French Paul's people—were shooting right over them!"

"Nobody got killed," Double-O replied dryly. "Only one guy hit. And the State Department must be very glad he isn't dead. He might tell them what other spies came in."

"Did you see the girl when you were at head-quarters?"

"Yes," he said.

"Is she . . . ?"

"Nice? Yeah. Pretty? And then some! Look, chick. Are you in love with the guy?" Double-O put his worry on the table, like a card it hurt to play.

When she didn't answer, he shook his head sadly and turned to repeat his question. She was laughing!

"Love Martin Burke?" she said. "Me? I'm fond of him. I think he's marvelous. But I'm the restless type, Bill. I couldn't fall for some one like that. It would have to be somebody who loved bright lights all the time, somebody who could tango like dreaming, somebody who could keep a girl on her toes—not settle down with her."

Double-O blew a long, relaxed cloud of cigar smoke. "Don't know what gave me the impression—"

"Of course, you do! I enjoyed necking with him—he seemed so surprised! He can be one of my favorite men friends as long as he likes."

"The lucky guy who finally does get you," the gambler said, "is going to need his luck. How else will he figure you out?"

Connie dismissed the problem with a gesture. "I asked about Marigold Macey because I hoped she would be nice—and pretty—and I knew he

179

had some romantic ideas about me. I was kind of—embarrassed by it."

"She's the undergraduate's dream of what a gal ought to be, I'd imagine. If the professor is interested, he'll have competition . . ."

Connie thought about that—anxiously, it seemed.

He dropped into a chair, his long arms and legs sprawling. "It's going to seem funny, now—without the Maroon boys pushing on me."

"That," she said, "is the main reason I busted in on your morning reveries, Bill. You owe that guy a lot."

"I owe the professor *plenty!* It's funny! That's what my family wanted me to be. A professional man. A doctor or a lawyer or a teacher. Only—I learned the wrong things too young, where I started college." He considered that for a moment. "I owe the guy everything. And I've cooked up an idea about that. See what you think."

As she listened, her eyes grew bright . . .

Twenty-three:

IT WAS late afternoon. The professor had slept almost around the clock—with Bedelia's aid and protection. Protection from reporters, news photographers, numerous other visitors, telegrams, phone calls—an excited, impatient and to him, unfamiliar, world. When he appeared, she hurried him through his breakfast and sent him to the grocery store for a "few items" she said she had forgotten. He decided to walk.

The air smelled of pine smoke as he started home; another high had come in from the north-west—and time for it, too, he thought. He came to the vacant lot and what seemed to be the same ballgame was in progress. He stopped to watch for a moment, smiling rather forlornly, as a man might who was trying to imprint on his mind a pleasant spectacle he would soon see no more. One of the youngsters shouted, "It's *the professor!*"

The game stopped in mid-inning. They ran up to him.

"Is it true," one boy asked in excitement, "that you captured French Paul without even a gun?"

The awe was such as the professor had never before experienced. "Some day soon," he said, "if I'm around, I'll tell you all about it."

"Just us kids? *Promise?*"

He smiled at a freckled face. "It's a promise."

There were cars in front of Bedelia's house. One was a grey convertible and a girl sat in it.

"Hello, Martin!"

"Connie! What in the world . . . ?"

"Bill's inside—Double-O. And President Tolver."

"President Tolver!"

"They're having a conference. They threw me out. Also"—she smiled—"Bedelia said you'd be coming along—and I wanted to see you a second. Hop in!"

He put the paper sack on the ground, against the trunk of a poinciana tree, and sat beside the girl. Anxiety and amazement confusingly filled his mind. Why had Tolver come to Bedelia's house? What would Tolver think when he found the gambler there? And why had the gambler and his niece called, anyway? Probably to offer unwarranted thanks.

"I had lunch with Marigold Macey," Connie said.

He started. "I didn't realize you knew her!"

"I didn't. But I called her up. Nice girl."

Somewhere, in the log jam of his thoughts and emotions, the professor felt a lifting of painful stress. "You aren't—upset—about . . . ?"

Connie understood him. "Martin, I'm very fond of you, But what I'm in love with, I guess, is glamour. I know it doesn't exist—in my mind. I suppose I have to learn it doesn't, in my feelings—before I can care about just one guy."

He said, in a low voice, "Oh."

"Remember the first night I kissed you?"

He would never forget. He nodded.

"Martin, I think you need some advice."

"I need barrels."

"The man—not the girl—is supposed to do the kissing. To begin, anyhow. With a gal like Marigold—"

He flushed. "I know. Once—I—I—"

"Once isn't enough! That's my barrel of advice. And you better go in. They're waiting for you."

President Tolver was a man with reddish hair and light blue eyes. A very large man, but graceful—and gracious. A former science professor with an intuition for diplomacy and a talent for administration. He rose when the professor came out on the porch. Double-O occupied the settee with Bedelia. Between them, they strained its capacity.

"Burke!" the president said. "I tried to phone all morning! But Bedelia fenced you in. I wanted to be first to congratulate you—instead of last."

The professor swallowed. "I appreciate it, Doctor Tolver."

"Magnificent feat! Has the eyes of the whole country on the University! I suppose you're getting—offers—from everywhere—"

"He is," Bedelia said. "But he doesn't know it yet. I've kept him busy."

The president went on hurriedly. "—but I'd like to have mine among them, Burke. Your friend"—he nodded toward Double-O—"has made the University a most generous gift. Insists it be anonymous. It will enable us to establish at once a tip-top department in your subject. Naturally, we'll offer you the Head. Your salary, as a Department Head, would be doubled."

The professor looked at the gambler. He swallowed harder. "That—that is—damned fine of you . . ."

Double-O's adzelike eyes moved out toward the variegated foliage—a stagey green in the last, level bars of sunlight. "Mighty little, considering."

The professor struggled for composure and said to the president. "I'd expected that—my notoriety —would make me undesirable as a faculty member. Quixotic folly!"

"Notoriety! Great heavens! Fame is the word for it! Not Quixotic, man! Homeric!"

"I'm grateful for the offer. And also for the confidence you showed in me, Doctor, when Mac-Falkland and the others were 'explaining' me in the Sunday magazine sections."

"I never believed that rubbish," the president said.

"I deeply appreciate the fact. But I can't teach."

"Can't teach?"

All three people were astounded.

184

He went to a chair and sat down. He stared at the floor for a moment. "Don't you understand? I have lost my faith in my own scientific position." He had to clear his throat. "I was a believer in intellect. In pure reason. My career was postulated on that. I held crime to be, in essence, a symptom of inferiority. It was an axiom of my lectures. But —in the past three weeks—" he sighed unevenly.

"You found it different," Double-O said mildly.

"I found it different. Ingenious. Imaginative. Resourceful. Highly organized. Skillfully employing the most modern techniques. Anything in the world but stupid!"

"Nevertheless," President Tolver put in shrewdly, "you succeeded in trapping them. A man with a higher education, but no experience whatever in their environment. Doesn't that clinch your hypothesis?"

The professor leaned back in his chair. His body seemed lifeless. He shut his eyes. Only his voice had a spark. "On the contrary. I used very little intelligence. Cunning, yes. But what motivated me? What forced stratagems into my consciousness? *Emotion.* Pure *emotion!*"

Bedelia said, "Rats, Martin! Harmon himself thinks you're headier than any of his own men!"

"Consider the facts, not Harmon's flattery," the professor answered. "Why did I think—at the start of this whole business—of mailing the money back to Double-O here? Because I was infuriated at the idea of being robbed! Why did I note the

185

marl on the tires of the sedan and seize a handful of frond ends? Because I was determined to revenge myself on that fat Alsatian, if I could!"

He leaned forward, now, and scowled at them. "Why didn't I give the evidence to the police, or the F.B.I.? Vanity! Egotism! Why did I spellbind Chuck with the data Double-O gave me? Because I was afraid to die—and stalling off the moment! Why did I think of the stratagem which got me out of that pesthole in Cuba? Because I was crazed with rage over what I thought was murder of Bedelia. Why—even at the end—did I risk Marigold Macey's life to find that launch? Because I had grown to detest the Maroon Gang with all my soul! Nothing of the abstract mind about it! Pure instinct produced such ideas as I had! And that is contrary to everything I have taught!"

There was a moment of silence on the porch. The last bar of orange sunlight faded and the evening was grey.

"Still," the president said, "when you've thought these things over, won't you feel that the social psychologist has a function?"

"Function?" Professor Burke hesitated. "Yes. He has the function of showing that the potentiality of what we call 'crime' exists in every human being. His function is to prove that crime is intellectual *disease*—not inferiority. That apathy toward evil is criminal! A college graduate needs to know more than merely to refrain from crime; he needs to be a lifelong crusader against crime! His emotions—his *instincts*—should be permanently aroused. And that, Doctor Tolver, is as much an inspirational function as a function of teaching. I am afraid such classes would scandalize many faculty members!"

The president, like the gambler, was looking into distances. "Has it occurred to you, Professor, that you're in an ideal situation to launch precisely such a course? A position that would—truly—inspire?"

"It will," Bedelia said, "when he reads his telegrams."

The professor looked incredulously at the president. "You mean, you'd stand for that sort of teaching?"

"We shall welcome it!"

The doorbell rang.

Bedelia looked at the watch on her fleur-de-lis pin. "That's the reporters. I told them to come at five thirty." She left the porch before the professor could reply. President Tolver announced the new appointment.

MacFalkland, accompanied by another man, called soon after the others had left. There was no boom in MacFalkland's voice. His hands trembled. He immediately—and nervously—introduced the stranger. "This is George Drufton, publisher of the *Inter-World Press*. The Sunday supplement that—appears in so many papers."

Professor Burke said, "Come in."

"My firm," said Mr. Drufton, "owes you amends."

The professor was feeling in a less somber mood. "I should say so!"

"I'm—hideously sorry—" MacFalkland began.

"So I suffer from overrepression!" The professor said, his eyes gleaming. "As a result, I am a bi-cerebral! What in hell is that, MacFalkland?" His colleague had turned scarlet; the publisher was fidgeting. "I am the schizoid type of renegade! My early childhood 'inclined me, by the law of con-troposite-neurotic-reflex'—to take up crime! *Gibberish!*"

"We realize," Mr. Drufton put in urgently, "that you have grounds for a damage suit, although we have stopped the series. Such suits, of course, are expensive."

Professor Burke now stared at the publisher. "I was 'dead'—so you weren't worried! Not even relatives to fight for my reputation! And Mac-Falkland here—dreaming up that half-baked psychological explanation of how I came to be a smuggler! I should say I have a suit! However, I won't sue. Rest your minds about that."

"Won't sue?" the publisher repeated, unbelievingly.

"No. All I ask is that Mac here attend my lectures for the next few months. As my subordinate, he has a lot to learn."

"I must say," the publisher murmured, "that's generous!"

MacFalkland seemed to choke.

Professor Burke walked over to him and slapped his back. Slapped it mightily. "Buck up, old boy! All you need is to get out in the world more!"

"There was another matter—"

The professor turned to the publisher. "Yes?"

"No doubt you are getting offers for your life story. I mean—the real story . . . ?"

"Bedelia says so. I haven't looked into it yet."

The publishers seemed cheered. "I see. Well, in view of the fact that my supplement has such immense circulation, and was the medium which made so many misstatements about you—"

"Misstatements!"

Mr. Drufton glanced at MacFalkland in a pained way. "Whatever you wish to call them, Professor. I deeply regret it. And I am eager to buy your story. Appearing in my supplement, it would undo the harm that's been done. I will pay twenty-five thousand dollars."

The professor's voice was high. "Twenty-five thousand dollars!"

"Don't accept," Bedelia called, marching unabashedly into the room. "You already have an offer for thirty."

"Thirty-five!" Drufton said instantly.

She smirked at him. "We'll let you know. Now, gentlemen, it's far past dinnertime—and the professor has an engagement at eight thirty."

The professor sat at the dining-room table. "Thirty-five thousand dollars . . . !" he muttered wildly.

Bedelia served soup. "Figure out the income tax, before you get too elated."

"What engagement have I at eight thirty?" he asked, after tasting the soup.

"I told Marigold you'd be over to see her."

He drove the shadowy blocks swiftly.

"She's in the garden," Marigold's mother said. "Isn't it kind of chilly?"

"The barbecue fire is burning. And the house is full of people who want to meet you. So she went out there, when she heard your car."

The fire made some light and a considerable warmth. She was standing beside it. "Hello."

The professor did not stop to reflect that he was following instinct rather than reason. He gathered up the girl and proceeded along the lines suggested by Connie Maxson.

"I trust," he finally said, "you won't mind being a professor's wife."

Her curls shook—horizontally. "Nope."

"Because if you did mind, you'd just have to bear it, somehow."

"Martin."

"Yes?"

"Will you promise not to hunt criminals again?"

He considered. "It seems unlikely I ever will. But promise? No. I won't promise."

Martin Burke had found himself. Intuitively,

he knew it. He always would know—now. It satisfied her and she put the satisfaction in simple words. "I guess you're boss—"

"You're darn right I'm boss!"

Their silhouettes became a unit which threw a complex shadow on the grass.

Impatiently, the judge strode to the hedge and leaned through the opening. They had stepped off the lawn and his pineapple was menaced again. He started to protest, grinned instead, and turned back to the house. His guests could wait. And the hell with the pineapple.

Professor Burke's first class of the new year was held, at the request of President Tolver, in Memorial Hall and attended by the faculty, by reporters, and by certain guests, among whom was a tall man with level grey eyes and his beautiful niece—a couple pointed out by hundreds. There were no absences among the regular students. All other undergraduates who could crowd into the hall were present. Bedelia sat on the platform.

"The topic of my last lecture," Professor Burke began, "was crime, vice and civic corruption. I am going to repeat that lecture because, since giving it, I have obtained new material on the subject."

The distinguished guests laughed. The undergraduates whistled and stomped.

Only Miss Orme—the student with ensnooded hair that resembled a beaver's tail and the firm life purpose of becoming a social worker—disliked the new course. It was too realistic, she felt: too harrowing—and not intellectual enough. Professor Burke had deteriorated, in her opinion. One day she entered his office to tell him so. She found him with Miss Macey in his arms.

"Come on in," he grinned at the shocked student. "Another branch of socio-psychology. Courtship. Fascinating study!"

Miss Orme fled, and in the next semester, changed over to economics.

www.ingramcontent.com/pod-product-compliance
Lightning Source LLC
Chambersburg PA
CBHW050731250626
47155CB00005B/1748